ALTERNATE BURN

ALTERNATE BURN

THE BURNER TRILOGY
BOOK TWO

MARIANNA PALMER

Red Empress Publishing
www.RedEmpressPublishing.com

Cover Design by Cherith Vaughan
https://www.facebook.com/coversbycherith

CHAPTER 1

You never really get used to danger. The same way you never get used to being able to ice something over with a mere flick of your finger. After years on the run, I still had my heart in my throat as I snuck around the corner of the large building. Large, ugly building. Stone, square, no real personality.

Maybe that's the reason why my heart leaped when I saw Redmond. He was around the other corner, watching the security cams above us. He was waiting for my signal. But his long lengths of wonderful blond hair were tied back into a braid. He had his perfect face pushed into concentration mode. His jaw was set tight, perfect lines underneath skin. This was going to be a battle. And I still wanted to rub my thumbs through his forehead and unwrinkle his wrinkles. The ugly building was a perfect contrast to his beautiful magnificence.

Focus…I had to focus. There was plenty of time for that later. And right now, there was more danger than I'd ever thought possible. Once I gave the signal, we'd storm the place. Explode everything in sight—that was Redmond and

Erin's specialty—and then ice the pipes to make the walls open. Me and Cindy.

Though I missed Bobby, who was back on the island with our newest saves, Cindy wasn't a bad addition. We were a regular team now.

"Be cautious," an annoying voice said in my head through the earpiece I wore. Oh, yeah. An idea from our new mentor and leader, Natalie Larson. We were constantly connected. She was staying back. Not enough firepower—or ice power in her anymore. Lost over the years. "We need to destroy this place, not go to war."

I rolled my eyes. *Wonderful.* It was better when I was the only one in my head.

"Got it," I hissed. I gave Redmond the okay signal, and he swung his arm back. His elbow high in the sky, he unwound a fire whip and snapped it in the air. It burned through the cameras above us. As expected, the alarms went off.

"Here they come," Erin said in my ears. She was usually a pessimist. But in this case, she was right.

Like a bunch of roaches, Breathers roared out of the building. I've never gotten used to those things. Unnatural monsters that came from some dark hole. They had hunted me since childhood. Super-strong, super-fast, and practically invincible. I stayed back as Redmond and Erin took them on. Natalie had supplied us with *lots* of explosives.

The trick to defeating Breathers was to use natural fire. And fuel with Burners' stuff. My fingers itched as the Breathers fell.

Pow!

Guns slamming through the night. And I stayed under cover. The worst thing I could do. But I had to. Like Natalie said, we were after information, nothing else. The proof of it all was in this building. Where the Burners were. Where the Breathers were bred. And where the leader of this evil organization made their home. So much to gain. Next to me, Cindy tensed.

"Slow now," I whispered. "Our friends have gotta get them away from the building."

Erin jumped into the night sky, brought her arm down onto a Breather's head, and then spun around him into a headlock. Redmond roared into battle, and then both ran, making faces.

"Come on, try and get our scent!" Erin called. Then she took off, Redmond right behind her. I didn't know how many Breathers were inside, but we had to take the chance.

"Now!" I ordered. Both of us felt for the water in the pipes inside. Wonderful thing, indoor plumbing. No site was truly secure as long as it had modern conveniences.

Strange. Where was the water?

"Third biggest?" Cindy asked. I glanced at her. She wasn't even furrowing her brow. She knew exactly where the most extensive water was. "Ice it to a fountain?"

I just nodded. I didn't know why I couldn't feel it.

Oh, there it was! You silly elusive water, you. My old friend, why are you avoiding me?

"Come on, baby, work with me," I whispered.

The water exploded from inside, making a humongous hole. "Let's get in there. What we're after is paperwork."

I ran through the hole. Looked left and right. I wished I had eyes in the back of my freaking head! I hadn't ever gotten over being hunted. It had been months since the last time, but I could still feel the sinister intentions permeating this building.

But, yay! No one inside. The security, what little there was of it, was outside chasing Redmond, which filled me with a different source of dread. I just found him. Had fallen in love. And he could be taken away from me so easily. If I had known I'd be putting others into danger when I went back there, I'd have stayed on the safe island.

We walked through the building like we owned the place. I wondered how truly badass we looked. I'd never have admitted it before, but I wanted to know I looked cool walking through these halls with my black leather jacket with red stripes on the side and my white hair braided down behind me. I wore a tight shirt, which Redmond had said looked very nice and then positively drooled. Pants that were nice and tight. I'd bet I looked like a supermodel. And, no, I wasn't just saying that.

It was all part of our attack, if I was being honest. Natalie had suggested it. Our first form of defense was our beauty, catching anyone who looked at us off guard. When you have a weapon, you exploit it.

"Why paper?" Cindy asked.

"Hmm?" I asked. Another explosion outside just as I made a living snake of water break through the hall in front of us. We had a vague idea where the file room was. I didn't know what kind of place this was. It looked like an office building with all these cubicles I was tearing through, freezing them. Leaving little ice sculptures of Greek gods that I'm sure the owners of this place wouldn't appreciate upon return. Fun, huh? With all the time off, I had discovered a new hobby, ice sculptures. I couldn't believe how much making art with something I had hated all my life gave me such peace. It also left an impression on my enemy. My ice wouldn't melt unless they took a flame thrower to it. I was leaving my mark.

"This is the digital age!" Cindy continued. "It seems stupid to have them all paper."

I didn't agree. "Possible file interruption. Hackers. Security. Natalie is good at hacking into computers, so…"

Cindy laughed. What did she think this was, a walk in the

park? I was glad Erin was in her life, give this bubbly pile of optimism a little seriousness. She too looked like she was ready for her close-up. Her black hair shined under the unnatural light overhead. She wore a red jumpsuit with gaps in certain places to reveal skin. She looked like a Japanese goddess strolling through our reality.

Cindy pushed office chairs out of her way by bumping up ice mounds under them.

"Nothing so far!" she said with a grin. "But look!" Far across the way, there was a door that had no sign or anything to announce that it was something more. "I'd bet it's in there!" she said in a singsong voice.

Bubbling over. A coffee pot on overdrive.

"Sure." I whipped my hand out to create another ice sculpture. Nothing came. I shook my head. Cindy kept going. I decided to hold off on my personal ice museum and ignore the horrible feeling in the pit of my stomach. Something was wrong. It had been since I left that machine that tried to take my essence away from me. I was just glad this looked like it was going to be a quick and easy mission.

The door led to, as Cindy assumed, a room full of files. Large white filing cabinets. The floor was bare concrete. No windows marred the walls.

"Oh, wow, I love humanity!" Cindy crowed, pointing to little placards on every single filing cabinet. "They like organization!"

"We're humans," I said. I think I sounded tense. Cindy quickly changed tactics.

"Okay, then, Breathers...Oh, and the humans who control Breathers. This is easy! Look."

I rushed over to one and gestured to the door. "Watch the entrance."

"Aren't we going to take all of them?"

"No," a strong voice said near my ear. I jumped. I wasn't

expecting Redmond to come up next to me. He placed his heavy hands on my shoulder, soothing my nerves. He could always tell when I was going to start freaking out.

"Right," I said. "We're going to look, take what we can, and…"

"Burn the rest," Erin put in. She too had entered the room silently.

"The Breathers?" I asked without daring to breathe.

"Trapped under a burning car. Silly things followed us into traffic," Erin answered without even a mark of a smile.

I turned back toward the filing cabinet I was in front of. It was labeled "Origins." I pulled it open. I heard the others doing the same. I read as fast as I could. Just because the security here was stymied didn't mean we were safe. There was always backup. I was hoping no Flyers guarded this place.

Origins…I was right! The addresses of places that held Breather breeding grounds. That was a pretty piece of information we had been lucky to verify. Breathers weren't born naturally, they were bred. And the last thing we Burners needed was more of them.

"Check!" I said and grabbed the files, shoving the folders without care how they smushed into the bag over my shoulder.

Erin and Cindy found where the next generation of Burners was and didn't look at the folders long, just doing what I did.

"Laoni?" Redmond said. His voice was shaded, as if he wasn't sure if I should know something.

"What?" I joined him across the room. The outside lights flickered from the still burning fires.

"Your last name is Kekoa, right?"

I nodded.

"Here's a folder on you. It makes no sense. Why you?"

There was no time for this. "Just bring it. We'll deal with that..."

Suddenly, Natalie's voice hissed in my head. "Flyers. It's what I was afraid of. Your little war has gotten the wrong kind of attention. Get out of there. Now! Travel south. They're coming from the north. Move!"

Her voice, sketched by years of danger, was tighter than normal. We didn't need more motivation. We just ran. Back the way we had come. Redmond and Erin left a trail of fire. A long tongue that licked up every piece of metal and trace of paper. We wouldn't be able to use it, but neither would they. They had lost years of information. That's why you should always have backups, people!

Redmond grabbed my hand and held it as we jumped together over a downed cubicle wall. "Nice sculptures."

I tried not to smile.

"Death! Danger!" I scolded, and we tore the back wall open. We were out in seconds. But I heard the sound I had grown to listen for. Flyers didn't make much noise. But there was a little hiss that came with them. Like a flying snake.

They were close.

"This way!" I yelled. We disappeared into the forest.

Mission accomplished.

Around the corner, Natalie had the most unassuming automobile possible, an old-fashioned Volkswagen bus from the sixties. The windows were, of course, covered in curtains, and inside was lots of equipment. We piled in, sat on our seats, and Natalie pulled away.

I couldn't believe it when she yelled, "Seatbelts!"

We, like good kids, ignored her. There were more dangerous things out there. I reached toward Redmond's bag, brushing his chest as I did.

"Ooh, now, Oni?" he asked, misinterpreting my

wandering hands. "We have company." He kissed the top of my head. I elbowed him.

"Later, Mond. I just wanted to see my file. Like, am I enemy number one? The worst Burner, destroy at all costs?"

Mond chuckled and held me close. He watched Natalie drive back to our hideout as I opened the file. What I saw surprised me.

I dropped the folder. Then I held my hands over my eyes like I was a child and just had a nightmare. The file wasn't on me. It wasn't really about me. Only one line was. I was right about destroy at all costs. But there was something else more important.

"What is it?" Mond asked.

"My mom…I know where she is. I know where another Burner is. My sister."

I couldn't see for the rest of the trip.

CHAPTER 2

*D*ear Diary,

I don't want to forget to write. This time I'm more surrounded by people than ever before. We've just left the submarine. Not the one from the last time I wrote. This one is going out, leaving us alone. A whole slew of Burners on board. Yes! We saved them. We did. Natalie, Redmond, Erin, and Bobby. Oh, and me. I don't really know how to admit that. On one hand, I feel arrogant, saying how much a part of it all I was. But in the same breath, I've gotta tell the truth.

Anyway. Yes. Diaries are fun! I go off the main point. Talk about my silly emotions. Okay, back to the facts. The surprise? Cindy. She followed us on one of the trips to the island, surprising all of us. That girl can shadow people!

We were getting to be too big of a group for sneak attacks, so after we saved the six Burners on the way to be slaughtered...I'm overexaggerating again, aren't I? They were heading toward a new facility. These creepy Breathers had lined them up and were marching them through a forest.

We attacked.

I have to admit it was fun. Not like the last life or death battle.

I even struck a stinking Breather straight on his head. Caused him pain. Who knew I could do a concentrated ice beam that wouldn't catch a scent and would hurt the Breather? It was great!

Am I a monster? I hate those things so much! I want them dead. But, should I exult about their pain?

Hmm, absolutely. Definitely.

Back on topic. Bobby's gone now. I'll miss his non-stop talk about bugs, but he volunteered to get the six Burners to the island. He knows the submarine in and out now, and we have Cindy. Yay!

I don't mind her. I used to have a problem with her hero worship. But, now? It's not so bad to have someone around who trusts your every order. It's just the fact that we're two couples here. Lovestruck, free couples who have never even dated. Natalie rolls her eyes a lot these days but says nothing. She doesn't tell us what to do except when we go into battle.

For me, though, I am in charge. And Cindy says, "Yes, my captain; anything, my captain." But she sometimes defers to Erin, who defers to me, thankfully, but I...

Yes. I'm nervous. She's my friend. They all are. I have almost too many these days. But to have someone blindly follow me? I'm the leader!

And I'm whining. I guess now that we've been freed, I can be normal. This diary...sheesh! I've read what I've written. Where's the "agh! I'm going to die" thoughts? We're soooooooooo not out of danger here.

Still...dates are nice. Natalie does research with her big old computer as we slip into other areas of the building to try and pretend we're going out to the movies. Mond and I, we're doing great. He is my world. He has the cutest little mole behind his ear. I found that out by exploring. And when I kiss it, he makes the cutest sound too...

Oh! The place we are! The facts, the freaking facts. I'm not droning on and on in my diary for my emotional state. I'm trying to do this for records. After we said goodbye to the new

Burners, Bobby, and the submarine, we rode a city bus—a nasty experience—together to a junkyard. Natalie is handy with cars and spent a night fixing an old Volkswagen bus. Mond hotwired it to start without a key, and we drove it to a new headquarters. Not nearly as nice as Natalie's Bed and Breakfast. Not...even... close. I think we drove as far as Louisiana. I'm still really bad at geography. When water surrounds us, we still are protected from the scent of the Breathers. But we have to endure the most muggy summer I've ever known. It's like I'm walking into a warm bath every time I leave the hidden building. Yeah, it's hidden. Almost sunk down into the muck. Think little green creatures teaching the force and you'll get the idea of what it looks like.

It's bad even for people who don't care about temperature. Yeah, we've still got the miracle clothes that regulate our powers, thank goodness. Sometimes I just throw them all off, though, and I can still feel the wraparound of moisture even as it turns into ice and falls at my feet.

Mostly, we've been waiting.

Mond and I sometimes double date—if that's what you can call it—with Erin and Cindy. We make up our own distractions. Bowling across a swampy marsh isn't only irritating, it's pointless too.

Sorry, I'm being petty. Bowling was voted on over my wonderful idea of freeze basketball. I'd make a ring, and they'd try to throw ice into it. Mond liked it. Erin hated it. And, of course, Cindy sided with Erin. But what really decided it was that Mond and Erin were more comfortable with fire. Which meant it'd be one-sided.

So, we made up balls of woven swamp grass and tried to bowl them into pins made from the same.

There were no movies to watch. Nothing to do! And if we dared leave, we'd have to watch for the purple eyes of the Breathers, which only serves to remind me we're still in danger.

Face it, I could have stayed on the island. I signed up for this. But why does it have to be so boring?

Oh, I'm blathering because I've got another issue. Oh, Diary, it's so silly. I don't even want to put it in here.

It's nothing. Really. I think. Okay, fine. I burned a piece of Mond's skin. I was kissing him quite hard on the neck, and he made a sound like "oomph," but he drew me into his arms and said nothing. We just finished the night, but I looked at his neck the next day and there was a hickey. But worse, it was a burn.

No, I'm sorry. It was silly of me to bring it up, Diary. I'm just making a big deal of it. I just used my teeth. I must have. I couldn't burn him. No way. He's the fire. I'm the ice. And we're more than compatible.

At the same time, if I can't be honest in here, where can I be? I think I burned him. How is that even possible?

It's the outfits. It must be. My powers are regulated, but what are the side effects of long-term use? I've gotta ask Natalie if she's studied it at all.

Where was I?

Right! Natalie says she's following a lead that will tell us where to go next. Hurray! I want more action.

Yes, me. The girl who has been hunted since she was young. I guess I'm more used to that than peace and quiet. What does that say about me? I'm happier with fighting and running. I just never learned to do anything else. The only time that was peaceful was when I was at the facility, and that still fills my brain with what Erin said once. "Like sheep to the slaughter."

Yes, peace brings slaughter. There, I admitted my ultimate problem. I'm scared of peace because I know strife and war are just on the other side.

～

*J*ust came back from a debriefing. It's go time. Erin's words. No more fun. No more dates. We're heading to a place that is filled with documents. A goldmine of information that will help us.

Strange, I feel so weird inside. Premonition? Paranoia?

Or maybe it's just that wonderful meal that Natalie made us of bean burritos and cream soda. Bad combination.

I'm ready. We're going. See you when I get back. Funny, I have a place to leave my diary. I don't have to carry it in my backpack. When did this sunken building become a home? Too weird.

CHAPTER 3

I stared out the window of my room. The water lapped at the window but didn't come in. Completely watertight.

I wanted to cry some more, but I couldn't. I didn't know how to feel about learning I had a sister, a Burner like me. One who Mom kept.

Yep, she kept her. And my sister was the next target.

A knock on my door. I knew who it was. "Come in, Mond," I said, and he walked in. I couldn't shake him. I didn't want to. I just told him to leave me. Good boy, he ignored me.

"You doing okay?"

"I don't know what to do. We've gotta save her. They'll go after her. But I almost don't even want to go. I might see Mom. I'll take away her daughter, at the very least. Gem, that's her name. Her powers are latent. At least, the report says so. She's ten. Ten. Six years younger than me. That means Mom had her *after* she threw me out. Fun!"

Mond pursed his lips. "This bothers you."

"No duh."

"I don't get it," he said and slipped down onto my bed next to me, letting our shoulders touch. It was nice. But... uncomfortable. Bad position, I guess. I shifted, trying to get comfortable. "The witch threw you out. You should have given up on her."

I crossed my arms and pouted. Hey, no danger! I could be petulant all I wanted. "I have! I'm just angry. Why did *Gem* get to be kept? Does Mom not know? Or maybe..." I caught Mond's raised eyebrows.

"Okay! Fine. I'm not over it. It feels like crap to know Mom kept a sister of mine but gave me up. I want to know why. I want to find out. But you know what we'll do. We'll go in, grab her, and then send her off to the island."

"Or...you could find out. I wouldn't judge. We could go together."

I wanted to get closer to him, but I was just so uncomfortable. I shifted again, then stepped to standing. "Natalie won't allow us. She wants us to stay together until she tells us what to do. She's checking out everything. Last I heard, Natalie said that my sister is in a 'waiting zone,' whatever that means. They won't bother her, which means our first target will probably be a Breather breeding ground. Any day now."

Mond stood too. "Any week, actually. I checked the address. Your mom and sister live in Baton Rouge. Not far. Easy drive. We go. You talk to your mom. It'll be like old times."

Did I catch a glimpse of wistfulness in his tone? "You miss it? Being alone. On the run, just you and me?" I asked.

He surprised me and nodded. "Yeah. I'm not so sure about this whole team thing. Even before, I wasn't much of a joiner. But I do like it. I just need a few days. Days where I'm doing something, not sitting around waiting. I feel like I want to explode, but there's no reason. I need to *move*."

I grinned and took his hand, swinging it as I walked up to lean on him. "Ah, so self-sacrificing. Making it sound like it's for me, but it's for you."

"But of course!" he joked. "I don't want you to have any closure. Look, I'd stay forever in this building if it was good for you, you know that."

I nodded. I did know that. He was the one thing I could count on. The one who saved me from running. The one who saved everything. "You do know we might get in the way of Breathers? It will be dangerous, and no team to watch our back."

Mond laughed. "We did pretty good on our own. Once. Besides, it's just a recon mission. Nothing else. We'll lay low. And if we get Gem and bring her back, it'll be one less mission the team has to go on, right?"

I couldn't help it. He was tempting me. I wanted to know more. I wanted this to be more than just a saving mission. I was curious what happened to Mom. I still thought about her sometimes when the night came around. Wondered what she looked like now.

"We'll go. When?"

"When Natalie's distracted by planning the next move."

"Oh, so any time in the daylight hours. Gotcha."

First, though, we had to endure dinner together. I didn't like being required to eat with everyone. Natalie insisted. Maybe because we were the only family any of us had left. Erin still talked about hers. It had been so long since she'd seen them. They probably thought she was dead. Mine, I didn't want to think about even with the recent developments. As far as I knew, Natalie only had her twin sister, Nora. Mond's family was either dead or he *really* didn't want to talk about them. Cindy was quiet about anyone she left behind. She missed them so much it hurt, so it was easier for her to forget it.

The thing was, now that we were all free from the facility, the obvious thing for everyone to do was what I'd planned to do—look up family. But they were consumed with the mission. I never liked sitting still. No guilt could even reach my mind. I blamed it on the years of running. I did what I needed when I needed. And I needed to see what my mother was doing. Did she have the million dollars now? Or did she, I don't know, gamble it all away or drink it down her throat? Vices? Or was she responsible? I didn't know I had this many questions about her.

I had said goodbye when I realized she'd never come to pick me up. I thought I was done. But she had grown inside me. A piece of my soul would never be happy until I knew. Did she regret giving me up?

"Hey, where the hell are you?" Erin said with a scowl. I glanced up to see her looking at me expectantly. In fact, everyone at the table was.

"Umm, here? This is wonderful, Erin. I didn't know you could cook."

She rolled her eyes. "Yeah, great, thanks. I boiled water, stuck noodles in, and tossed it together with chicken and spices. Yay. Can you give me the gosh-darned salt!"

I blushed. I wasn't used to people yet. She must have been asking for a minute or so. I grabbed it from the side of my elbow and tossed it to her. She caught it in midair. Even during this peaceful dinner, she was primed for battle. Her lovely crinkly hair fell down to her shoulders, making an ad for shampoo. Her eyes were sparkling, and her stunning brown face shined like a star.

Everyone around me was digging in. I guess Erin had taken over the kitchen before Natalie could pull out the canned stuff again. I hadn't been lying. It was nice to have a homecooked meal instead of all the processed stuff Natalie had managed to get here.

Made sense. We couldn't order in. And going to the store was way too dangerous. The Breathers were on high alert these days thanks to the facility we had torched. Oh, and the fact that we kept stealing Burners out from under their noses.

"What's next, Nat?" Erin asked. "Are we going to go after *her* sister or what?"

Natalie wound six strands of spaghetti around her fork and stuck it in her mouth. "No, we're not. I think it's too dangerous."

I caught Mond's eyes, who gave me a secret grin. We were going to face that danger. But it'd be a lot easier for two than four.

But still...I did wonder what the danger was. One woman. My mom. One Burner. And the house being watched, I guess. But still. Breathers didn't hurt humans. That meant we could easily go in the daytime and keep lots of innocent bystanders in our way. Easy.

But I noticed Natalie didn't look at me. Maybe I should have read through those files more myself. I had only glanced. "Why?" I asked. "What's the danger? Are there lots of Breathers watching?"

Natalie gave me a smile. She was still looking out for me. I couldn't help but smile back. Natalie had taken on a motherly role since I met her. Nothing had changed.

"It's useless right now. The girl is not showing any talents. She must be latent. Not a threat or an aid, no matter who her sister is." She poked the corner of a cloth napkin to her chin to wipe up some sauce from it. "I'd say we just hole up here for a week. According to the files, they have Breathers staked out all around here. After that, we can move, and they'll be less ready to strike. We'll head down..."

Great, we had gotten her talking about the mission. I quickly interrupted. "Hey, how about we talk about something else? Like…" My mind blanked. I had *zero* clue what to talk about. I scanned my brain for a subject that we used to discuss the last time I was just friends with everyone and there was no danger.

Erin interrupted. "Like what? This is our life, Laoni. We fight. Wait. Fight again. There's no life other than this."

Cindy giggled and took her hand. "Now, that's not true. Come on. We'll end this someday."

Erin's eyes softened. But it was hard for her to lose her pessimism. I guess this wasn't exactly what she had signed up for when she waged her war. She probably thought she'd just go back home. But it wasn't safe.

I felt like a hypocrite. Here we were, trapped by a war none of us wanted, but I was going to go home—or to my mom. Whatever. I was going to listen to only my rules. And who cared about anything else?

I wasn't sure I liked being part of a bigger team. I couldn't just think about myself anymore. "Hey, what happened to your family, Erin? Can we visit them?"

Natalie's eyes snapped toward my face, a warning in them.

Erin snorted. "I have no clue! They loved Tampa, so they're probably still there. But…"

"But," Natalie put in before she could finish, "that is a huge city. And we will not be going there. Probably ever. It's too dangerous for her to go home. It's too dangerous for any of you."

Funnily, her eyes settled on me, as if she could read my mind. But I knew she couldn't. Her only telepathic abilities were with her twin sister. "So, are we supposed to just forget them?" I demanded.

Natalie pushed her chair away. "I'm tired." She stood up and looked back only once. "They forgot you. Reappearing in their lives would only bring more pain. And, worse, they might become casualties. The Breathers may not be able to kill humans, but Flyers don't care. At this time, we're not safe, and neither is anyone around us." Then she finished her escape. I didn't know what she was going to do tonight. I didn't much care. I was going to find my mom. I was going to ask her questions. Hey, I did quite well with my life before Natalie came along. She was never there my entire life on the run!

"This is our family," Cindy put in, trying to smooth my ruffled feathers. She could tell I was upset. "It's changed, you know. We all had families before. But life stole them away from us."

Mond snorted. "I think the Breathers had something to do with that."

Cindy shot him a withering stare. She and Mond didn't get along real well. He'd had a normal enough life away from the facility. She didn't know how abnormal his life was, or how he still had nightmares about the night his father hit someone while driving drunk and Mond's powers had sent them all to an early grave, making him go on the run. Mond didn't want anyone but me to know, and I wasn't going to betray him.

"So," I said slowly. "What's up for tomorrow?" I had to make sure everyone thought I'd still be here. Not driving down the highway as fast as Mond could drive the bus.

"Tomorrow?" Cindy asked. "I'm going to get back to drawing. I am itching to do some manga. I've got a good story with you as the main hero!" She pointed at me.

I hit my head into my hands even as Erin snarled and jumped up. She never like Cindy's hero worship of me. Erin would never admit it, but she wanted Cindy to worship her and her alone.

"Hey, Erin!" Cindy said and ran after her. Mond and I were alone.

Mond laughed. "This is a perfect soap opera, you know. Too bad Cindy doesn't have a real crush on you, or it'd only be funnier."

"Shush. Cindy has always liked me. But she *loves* Erin. Too bad Erin's so stubborn."

Mond stood up to start cleaning the dishes off the table. Outside was getting dark. The swamp water was pushing against the window. And I wanted to get rid of this stupid clothing again. Since Mond was the only one in the room, I stripped, losing that feeling of heat.

Mond grinned and looked away.

"What?"

"I really like it here," he said. "Nice sights." I blushed, but I was pleased. I liked when he looked at me.

"Isn't the humidity getting to you?" I asked.

He shook his head. "No, not as much as you. I'm not sure Erin, Cindy, or Natalie are suffering. What's up anyway?" He placed the dishes in the sink and ran water on them. The kitchen and dining room ran into each other, so I just lounged against the chair, trying to make sure my skin didn't ice up what I sat on.

"I don't know. I just thought it was bad for everyone. Humidity and ice. Ugly connection."

"I guess it's not so bad for fire," he said. "I think Natalie is mistaken. She thinks by forcing us to stay together, we'll develop familial feelings. She wants us to bond. But that's stupid. I'm actually getting aggravated. I've never been a slow burn."

I laughed at his joke. But I knew what he wasn't saying. Whether we liked each other or not, you couldn't force family. We needed to be there for each other, earn respect, and then see if there were some bonds to be made.

And first, all of us had to get closure on who we were stolen from.

"When we get back," I stated, "I'm going to talk Natalie into getting each of them home. I'm going to prove that there is a connection to be had with our original families. Or that, if not, at least the bond can be cleanly torn away."

"Nice idea. Oh, man!" He jumped up and ran to the table and jumped up on top. He laid right on it and splayed his arms wide. "I can*not* wait to get the hell out of here."

I pulled his arm close to me and hugged it.

Yuck. It felt worse than the humidity. I pulled away, hoping he didn't notice. I couldn't help the weird feeling of discomfort that was coming every time I hugged him. I wanted to hold him. Touch him. But I couldn't understand why I was so hesitant.

I shook my head. "Are you sure we shouldn't go tonight?"

He turned toward me and grinned. "Nope. Natalie will know. She gives herself the night off. I've been watching. She does some yoga to calm her mind. Then she sends off signals to her sister. Then she cries for half an hour. Then reads any book she can get her hands on. Then she goes to bed."

I just stared at him. "You've been planning this for a while. You really weren't planning on staying long, were you?"

"Oni!" he exploded a bit. "You feel it too. We were alone for so long. Now, we have all these others relying on us. We have this unending war. Remember, we wanted the island, not endless struggle."

I reached out and splayed his fingers, letting my pinkies stroke his knuckles. "I'm sorry. That was my fault. I dragged you into this. We could go back to the island. I'm sure a few others would gladly take our place. Bobby? Kenya? They'd love to get some action in."

Mond sat up and put his knee in a triangle as he stared at me. "But you wouldn't be happy. I was hoping you would.

But you seem…different now. After the machine they put you in, you're just so restless."

He was right. Great. I may not have asked Mond to come along, but I had forced him to with my own desires. I wondered how we could stay together. He wanted peace while I had always lived with war. What could we do about that?

CHAPTER 4

I don't know how to exist right now. I'm a part of a team, but Mond and I still seem to be on our own. There are so many people who are interested in me, who care about me, but how can I let them in? I'm a defector who constantly runs.

Even now, I don't want to stay here among them. I want to run again. I miss my tiny sewer home and the short time that Mond and I were happy there.

I miss the only thing to worry about being whether I'd die. Now I'm worried about everyone dying. These missions. The facilities we'll have to find. The new Burners who are so young and have to be shipped off to an island that is getting ever more crowded.

I mean, do they miss their old lives like I do? Did they want to grow up, go to school, grab a soda at the mall? We have these clothes that would make their journey to adulthood a lot easier than mine ever was. But we singlehandedly saved their future by destroying their present.

There are no stores on the island. No ways to order something online. They can't just hang out after school. Hell, there is no school. It's basically my own life with a tropical background.

It almost feels like I'm on the other side. Grabbing a group of Burners and forcing them where they need to go.

Natalie would tell me I'm being ridiculous. That we have no choice. And I know we don't. But some of them...they looked at me like I was a kidnapper. As if they had gone from the frying pan into the fire.

Maybe, after some time, they'll see. But I do understand. Really, I do! They were taken away from what they knew, only to be forced to go somewhere else. Bobby had actually picked up one of the young ones who was screaming and tossed him over his shoulder. It was all in the heat of battle, but what did that look like?

I wish I were on the island. I'd be bored, but I could explain to them what my life was like. How it was better to stay. It was better for their families if they didn't go back. It was better.

I'd be lying. Because I don't know that.

Agh! My heart is all over the place right now. Maybe it's because of what I'm doing tomorrow. I'm afraid of what I'll find. I don't know what the freak I am! I am stopping now.

I can't write. I can't sleep. I'm going to stare out the window and try to stop this miserable humidity from getting to me. Goodnight, Diary.

CHAPTER 5

The morning was thick with moisture. My lungs didn't like it. Funnily, it was making me miss my sewer home! That had been a disgusting, ill-concealed entrance to waste, but it was *dry*. Mond laughed when he saw my expression.

"You could go nude again."

I hit his shoulder, lingering as I pulled my hand down his bicep. What happened before had been a fluke. I still really liked touching him. "Not likely. We've got a mission."

There was one road out of this place, long and winding and almost sunk into the ground. Natalie had put some serious tires on the bus, helping it go through the muck easily. We tiptoed out to the little garage next to the house. The trees towered over it. Some sort of insect was buzzing in morning gratitude.

Natalie was inside, looking over the files we had managed to get, making notes and muttering under her breath. Talking to Nora? Or herself? She wasn't letting anyone in. This was the perfect time. Erin was still asleep, a late riser as long as we weren't on a mission. Cindy was taking a shower. She adored showers. Especially when she had a bikini she could wear that stopped the droplets of water from freezing and hitting her.

That was one thing we had in abundance. Clothes that let our powers flow but didn't affect every element around us. With the stinking humidity, I'd trade them all just for a TV!

I slid into the driver's seat. I had to turn the steering wheel while Mond pushed us out. No roaring motor, thank you!

We had agreed on this, of course. But I thought Mond should be the one behind the wheel because I'd never learned to drive. The idea of having this many pounds of metal in my control kind of freaked me out. It was bad enough I had to steer it now!

"You sure you don't want me to push?" I asked, sticking my head out the window.

He pushed the back of the van and gave me a grin that melted my heart. "It's easy, Oni. Truly. Just steer."

I looked forward and turned the wheel as he pushed. I looked back a few times, hoping no one would be looking out at our escape. It all seemed so easy. We decided. We left. We were gone! Why didn't anyone notice?

Secrets were so easy.

We reached the overhanging weeping willows that blocked the entrance to our swampy home. For a while, all I heard was the sweep of leaves against the metal of the bus. It was a long row of trees, perfect for privacy.

Finally, the road showed, and I turned the wheel one last time to move, and sat back panting. I could stare down a sadistic Breather, but driving a car made my heart want to fly out of my chest. To my surprise, Mond got in the passenger side.

"Um, wrong seat," I said.

He reached out and held my hand. "You never learned to drive, right?"

I shook my head. "All the normal milestones in life were lost. You know that." I grew fascinated with his thumbs. We had been together for a few months now, but it still felt like the first touch. It was distracting me from what he was suggesting.

He lifted my hand and laid it on the wheel, holding it there with his pressure. My heart thumped. But not from where I was pretty sure this was leading. "Mond, we need to get going."

"You can drive."

Now I got it. "No! I don't know how. I'll crash."

Mond's face flickered, and I regretted my choice of words. "Sorry. I mean…" I breathed in and out.

"I'll teach you. Come on, Oni. What if something happens to me? We may need a getaway driver that's not me."

My breath stalled in my chest. I couldn't even imagine… "No."

"You never wanted to learn?" His wonderful gray eyes stared into mine. The drooping trees behind him gave a wonderful backdrop.

I tried to answer his question. Had I? Sure. Of course. I'd even had a silly imagination when I was in the facility. When I graduated, Farrell would give me a car, a hug, and send me off into the world.

Silly. That was, of course, before I realized that Farrell was far from the father figure he pretended to be and was going to kill me when I reached that age, *not* give me a car.

Still…"Yeah, I guess."

Mond laughed. "I know. I could tell. You send an envious look at Natalie every time she starts the bus. Plus, you really *like* me turning it on."

I groaned and slapped his fingers with my other hand,

but again I lingered. This was heaven. We were alone, and his touch didn't make me uncomfortable.

"I want to teach you. Consider it a birthday present. Just like the rest of this trip."

Now, *that* caught me off guard. Birthday? We had birthdays in the facility, but they weren't celebrations. The staff and the Breathers would perform the cake ritual almost like a funeral. They knew, even if we didn't back then, that every year brought us closer to death.

No matter what, they adored us. It wouldn't stop them from draining us dry and leaving us dead, but they didn't wish for it to happen.

That being said, my birthday in the facility wasn't exactly on my day. It was for everyone who was my age. There had only been one cake, and none of us blew the candles out. One of the staff would do that honor just so one child wouldn't be honored over the other.

"Umm, it's not my birthday."

Mond laughed. "Yeah, it is. You really should have looked over your own file a little closer. Right there in black and white. July 25. You are a Leo."

My blank stare must have been very attractive because he pulled my hand to his lips.

"You know, astrology."

I scoffed. "I'm not going to look toward the stars for answers. I just...I was born on July 25. I never knew that."

"At 8:01 exactly. That's why I thought it'd be nice for the only gift I could give you would be a trip to the person who brought you into the world. Had I diamonds, I'd lay them at your feet."

"I don't need diamonds," I said, but I felt weird. That meant I was now seventeen. I'd never really counted before. Mond cared enough to check. "Mond..."

He sighed. "You hate the idea. I should have known. I am so sorry…"

I cut him off with a kiss, pressing my fingers into the back of his head. We breathed each other's breaths for the next few moments.

"Ouch!" Mond suddenly yelled. He shook his head but leaned in again. I pulled back.

"What? What did I do?"

He pressed his lips. "You bit me, I think."

There was red on his lips. A blister bubbled up. I hadn't bitten him. As fast as I could, I changed the subject. Denial was wonderful. I needed it so badly right now. "Sorry! Got a little caught up."

Mond gave me a grin. The blister burst and disappeared. My imagination? Yes. Of course. I couldn't *burn* him. Not Mond. "Not a problem."

"That was a thank you," I said. "I did always want to learn how to drive, and the fact that you knew that…You are wonderful. Where do my hands go?"

Mond laughed. "A loaded question."

"Mond!" I groaned.

"Okay, okay. They say nine and three is the best position." He quickly transformed. He was so cute! Excited about teaching me what he knew. Though he lingered a few times when showing me where my legs went and my hands, he was a confident teacher. Going slow enough for me to get it, but fast enough that I didn't get bored.

I turned the key too far, pushed the bus too fast forward, shrieked out loud when I braked, but I was getting the hang of it. Mond kept a straight face until we made it to the end of the block and he took the wheel again.

"You're a natural," he said with a grin as he now had the responsibility of the bus. I fell back into the seat.

"Not what it felt like, but thanks. That was…Wow. I can't believe it."

Mond threw me a map. I found the directions to Mom's address. I didn't know why I hadn't realized she had moved. I mean, we once lived in New York. Now Mom—and Dad— lived in Baton Rouge. I hadn't brought Dad into my mind a lot. But I had to realize what came with Mom was the man who had sold me. Who had been greedy enough to take money over his daughter. But he hadn't even been there for me in the first place. I hadn't had a birthday party even before the facility. Dad was the reason why. It would have taken the attention off of him.

What was I going to see? The highway flashed past. Mond left me alone with my thoughts. If my parents were rich now, they'd have a mansion. Blood money. For their daughter.

Acid poured down my back. I just wanted to claw some- thing. What was I doing? Would they even care about me? This was a fool's mission. Any sister I had would be as against me as they were…

Then again, she *was* a Burner. Didn't that mean I had an obligation to get her away before they sold her too?

My throat was tight with tears. I had been so busy, I hadn't given myself the luxury of thinking about my parents for so long. The wound they had given me hadn't healed. I had just buried it under lots and lots of anger, fear, and pain.

Just thinking about them stripped all that away. I had never gotten any closure. That's why I needed to not only grab my sister and get her out of there, but I also had to see my parents and ask them if they thought about me as much as I thought about them.

"You okay?" Mond asked.

I nodded. "Always."

He didn't believe me. But, of course, neither did I.

CHAPTER 6

The house was a thing of beauty, tucked away far back from the street with a long straight driveway and lots of trees behind it. Four large white columns were on the elevated porch. The windows were shiny, freshly cleaned. The sky was blue behind it.

My stomach felt like raw tuna. This house was expensive. It wasn't poor. Mom and Dad had taken the money and moved far away from where I had grown up.

"Talk," Mond said. He had parked the bus on the opposite side of the street at a good angle. No one from the house would be able to see us, and neither would any of the neighbors. A residential blind spot, so we could sneak in.

"They profited!" I couldn't hold it in. "From me being taken away. Tortured. Chased. I was afraid for ten solid years while they've lived in luxury. I want them dead. Let's freeze them. Or maybe, let's burn them. As they sit there writhing in pain, I'll explain why they have to die."

Mond tried to take my hand, but he pulled it back as if he had been burned. He looked at his palm, but I was too anxious to think about him.

"We'll take my sister, then we'll be gone. They'll be dead. Where'd all their money be then!" My screams echoed throughout the bus. Mond reached out for me again. Somewhere inside, I knew I should calm down. This was…dangerous.

I let him touch me. I breathed ragged. "Sorry."

"Not a problem. You have a dark side. So do I. But you know we can't kill them."

I deflated. My anger was gone. I wouldn't have wanted to see Mom suffer anyway. Dad, maybe. But not Mom. Regardless, I wouldn't turn my powers on humans. Not unless I had to.

"Okay. Then, maybe we can hurt them a bit?"

Mond just shook his head. He pulled me over the gap between the seats and gave me his support and love without saying a word. In a flash, I realized what would have happened had Mom and Dad kept me. Or tried to. Farrell wouldn't have stopped. He would have kidnapped me like Erin. Even on the off chance that he would have given up, I would never have met Mond.

The stars aligned and had brought him to me. How could I regret that?

"I love you," I whispered into his neck. He kissed my hair and brushed it back behind my ears to look into my eyes.

"Back atcha," he responded. "Your call. How should we proceed?"

I stuck my knuckle into my mouth as I looked at the quiet house. There were two cars parked in front. Someone was home.

My eyes narrowed. "I still want to know what happened. In we go!"

I pulled courage from a place I didn't know existed. This went beyond life and death. This was acceptance or rejection. That was more painful than any wound the Breathers had given me. I wanted to look into my parents' eyes. Ask them if they ever felt regret.

If they said no and laughed in my face, part of me would crumple and die.

Mond followed me in. The gate connecting the fence around the house was open. I strode up the long driveway. I wondered if anyone could see me coming. Out of habit, I checked the trees, the bushes. I listened for any steps besides Mond's. I breathed in the scent of the trees around us. I wasn't sure what kind they were, but their scent was rich.

Nothing else was here, as far as I could tell. But I had to remember that they were under surveillance, at least according to the report I had read.

I froze when I saw the wind chime hanging on the porch. Hummingbirds flying around a little sun. Mom had given it to me. She once called me her little hummingbird. And she had been my sun.

I rushed past the columns. I was being stupid. I should have broken in under the cover of darkness. Surprised my parents in their bed. Sneaked around until I had checked every nook and cranny of this place. Natalie would be furious that I hadn't. But all I could think of was that once Mom had loved me.

My mind was that hummingbird. My sun was inside. If she turned dark on me, my world would crumble in space.

"Oni," Mond whispered as I slammed my hand down on the front door. "Laoni," he insisted again.

But I ignored him. The door flew open.

There she was. Older. Wrinkles around the eyes. Wow. Her beautiful black hair. Brown eyes, like swimming pools of sunset. She had just jeans and a white shirt tied over a thin-strapped camisole.

Her eyes widened. Instant recognition. I had been six the

last time I saw her. But I guessed my mane of white hair, which I had let flow freely today, was a giveaway.

"Mom," I said stiffly just to ensure she knew who I was.

She gripped the door and nearly fell. "Laoni!"

Then she rushed forward. I could feel Mond's tension behind me. But she wasn't attacking. She was hugging me! Gripping tight. Like I once did to make sure she didn't give me up. She didn't seem to be concerned about whether I'd freeze her now. Not like before.

"My little baby girl!" she cried, sinking to the porch and pulling me down with her. "You're alive. You found me."

I fell into a million little pieces. My wet tears tickled. I wished they were ice. Damn these clothes! My arms hung down. I couldn't return the hug. I could barely breathe.

Acceptance? Ha! This was worship.

I don't even know how long we sat there. But finally, Mom pulled away and pushed my hair away from my face. "You are so beautiful!"

"Trait of Burners." I sniffed half a dozen times, but I couldn't get my nose clear.

"This goes beyond. I don't care how beautiful you all are. You shine brighter than any of them." She fell on my shoulder. Her tears soaked me.

"Can we come inside?" Mond said. He swallowed nervously and looked back and forth. This emotional display must have been unnerving to him.

Mom jumped and looked up. Her eyes widened again, this time for a different reason. As I could attest, Mond could take your breath away. He was positioned against one of the columns like a Greek statue. Perfect hair flowing down and touching his shoulders. His eyes lit up the whole porch. We were both on the ground, so we could properly worship him. But for Mom, it was worse. Way worse.

Because she was human, she just sat there stunned.

"You'll get used to it," I assured. "This is my friend Mond. Um, I mean, Redmond."

"It's a pleasure," he said. His tone wasn't pleasant. He hated her. I guessed that was my fault. I'd made him hate her. "My previous question. Oh, come on. Get a hold of yourself!" He snapped his fingers a few times.

Mom got the glaze out of her eyes. "Oh, sorry! Yes, of course, you'd have Burner friends. Come inside. We can sit in the living room and talk." She grabbed my arm and pulled me inside.

Wow, she got over her Burner daze *fast*! Mond walked in and slammed the door behind him. He rushed from window to window. Checking for danger, I guessed. Like I should have.

Mom didn't pay any attention. She wasn't like any other mortal I had come across. Not only had she recovered quickly, she ignored the miniature sun zooming around the room.

Mom's living room was a wide-open place with tall windows and hardwood floors. A few lush carpets spotted the area, almost like a chessboard. A huge brick archway took the room into the kitchen. And there were pictures everywhere.

My sister was in them. A chubby cherub of a girl with pinchable cheeks and vivid coffee eyes. She was gorgeous. Definitely a Burner. But I didn't see Dad in even one of the frames. None of his jerky self lingering in any glass corner. Another man was there.

Good looking himself. Velvet cropped black hair with insanely brown eyes. Like stars were in them.

Had Mom chosen someone else?

"Where's Dad?" I asked as I sat down across from Mom. She jumped up and rushed over to my side. Holding me again.

"Gone. That rat bastard has been gone for a very long time."

"How long?" I demanded. I shot a look at Mond. He was making me nervous. This wasn't the time or place for it. "Sit down, please, Mond."

He gave me a tight look.

"Redmond," I said.

He sighed and walked across the big room in, like, three strides. Then he perched on the edge of an ottoman in front of an armchair.

"To answer your question, your father has been gone for ten years."

Everything fell around me. "You left him?"

"As soon as I let you go." She gripped my hand, making marks. It was a very good thing I could control my powers through these clothes. Maybe they weren't so bad after all. Otherwise, she'd be an icicle by now. "I searched for you. But they told me you were dead. I didn't believe it, but…"

I couldn't fathom any of this. Mom? She had looked for me? Talked to Breathers? The facility? What?

"I don't understand." I was frozen. Every emotion had gone on the defense. I couldn't believe it.

"I hated myself!" Mom said. "I hated every part of my being after you were taken away. We were given the million. Your father was celebrating. But I turned to ash. Only a week later, I went after you, trying to find clues. It wasn't easy. They are *very* hidden."

I couldn't breathe. Couldn't swallow.

"When I returned home, defeated, I moved out. I spent my life trying to find you. But…"

Whatever had stopped her remained a mystery.

Someone came barreling downstairs.

My sister was here.

CHAPTER 7

I had seen her name. That was all I knew about her. Gem. Pretty and sweet, the girl who had just run into the room and looked at us, confused about who we were. She was even prettier in person. Plump all over with wonderful dimples on her elbows. Long flowing black hair that looked like liquid silk. A nice round chin with sparkling eyes. She looked happy. I wondered if I ever looked like that.

Mom jumped up almost as if she were ashamed of me. But as I looked at her face, there was no shame there. So, what had happened? I couldn't have burned her. Not in these clothes, could I have?

Gem walked over to Mom. Our mom. "Um, hi," she said. Her eyes widened at Redmond. She thought he was cute. Yeah, so did I. He really was, too. "Mom, who are they?"

I wondered what Mom would do. Would she admit who I was? Did Gem even know about me?

"Gem, this is your half-sister."

Half? Wow, so Dad didn't even get another child with Mom. Cool. Did that mean that Mom had passed the Burner gene on? Or was that even how it worked?

Gem broke into a huge grin. "Cool. Cool. Cool!" She ran over to me and threw her chubby fingers around my waist. "I've heard about you. Though, you're supposed to be secret. Shhhh." She put a finger to her lips and hissed.

I had to laugh. She was so different from most Burners I had met. Me included.

"Yeah, a secret. Why?" I asked. My bitter acid darkened Gem's sunny tones.

Mom sighed, holding me close to her again. If she had been burned, she wasn't twice shy. That was for sure. "It's a long story. I wasn't even sure we'd ever see you again. The Breathers told me you were dead."

I gaped at her. How much did Mom even know?

She gave me a wry smile and ran her fingers through my hair, like I was still a little girl, combing the strands behind my head. Then she placed a gentle kiss on my forehead. "Laoni, I fought for years to find out everything. I know there is more on this Earth than normal people realize. I know…"

I shrugged out of her embrace. She knew! That *was* a laugh. "They tried to kill me. All of us. You sold me. You were too terrified of my touch to stop Farrell from taking me away."

Mom didn't deny it. Nor did she look indignant. Instead, the weight of a thousand wounds filled her eyes. "I hate myself for that. I was so scared. I can't excuse it. I can explain that it's like…If you get bit by a dog, you pull away fast, by instinct. You shake your hand. You do everything in your power to get the thing causing you pain off of you."

"So, Laoni is a dog?" Redmond spoke up, defending me. I should have expected it. But I understood.

Gem narrowed her eyes. "That's not what she meant. Don't you dare get mad at my mom."

Funny, I was the one who should have been defending

her. But I couldn't. There was just so much water under this bridge. And, I reminded myself, I wasn't here for that. I needed to get Gem to safety.

"We're not here for the past," I said stiffly. I wouldn't admit that the past was part of the reason I had come. "We need to get Gem to safety. She's on their radar. It's a long story, but I, and a few others, got some records that told me about Gem. They know about her."

I hadn't expected much, but I had expected more than just a small sigh from Mom. "I know. But they won't come after her. Her abilities are latent. The Breathers think they have the situation well in hand."

So, Mom didn't know that there was someone behind the Breathers. Someone who had made all this possible. A human organization. Mom didn't know everything. But she sure knew enough.

"We have company!" a voice boomed. A deep masculine voice. I turned and saw the third person in the pictures. The handsome man with starry eyes. It wasn't just the photos. His eyes glimmered, almost an unnatural brown.

"Drake, this is Laoni," Mom said quickly, "my daughter and her friend, Redmond. They've come to warn us about Gem."

"So, you're my mom's new guy, huh? How long have you been together?" I asked.

Of all the questions, I hadn't expected that one to embarrass my mom, but she blushed. "Ten years."

Oh. Right after my dad. Interesting. "Did you?" I asked. It was a silly question. My whole history had changed. I had no family minus the ones from the facility and Redmond. But it was somehow the most important question in the world if she had cheated on Dad.

"No. Drake was after."

I was confused. There was something more here. Something...

Bam!

Everything exploded. The ceiling collapsed inward and Flyers came smashing down.

I had let my guard down. I pushed a piece of ceiling off me and rolled over to Redmond. The sky showed through the massive amounts of dust and debris. His arm was out, but he roared upward, spiraling fire into the air. He didn't aim for the Flyers. He had learned his lesson a long time ago. The majestic trees came burning down, pulling a Flyer from the sky. But we were surrounded.

Three Riders and two others. I threw up an ice shield. It surrounded the entire living room—or what used to be—and I looked for Mom.

I coughed through the dust as I started digging. "Mom!"

Don't be dead. No...I just found you.

I couldn't think. I couldn't feel. An army was around me.

Suddenly, Drake was next to me. "Here," he said. "Use this. Your powers won't work. There isn't much water here."

I was confused by what he was handing me, a gun of some sort. But I shook my head. "Mom, where's Mom? Where's Gem?"

"I'll get them. You worry about getting out of here."

I had no time to argue. My ice wall burned down and fell into shards. I took aim, pulled the trigger, and...*Bam!*

It blew the Rider off his bike. With a huge hole in his chest, he flew across the sky, slamming into the trees. I turned around and fired again. The Flyer crashed down.

Oh, yeah. I could get used to this!

I fired again and again, taking them down. I ran over to Redmond, who was just staring, his mouth agape. "What the...?"

I laughed. "Here, sweetheart, go nuts. It's fun!" I kissed him and turned back to Mom and Gem.

I heard the gun go off a few more times. I ran over to Drake, who was dusting off Mom and Gem. He looked like some kind of doctor, checking over their wounds for any life-threatening injuries.

"They okay?" I asked.

He kept his face away. "Yeah. Just bruised."

"Looks like the Breathers found her." *I hated to say I told you so, but...*

"No, they found you. You shouldn't have come here in the daylight. You should have contacted us first. You almost got them killed." He turned his back to me and picked up Gem. She was crying softly into his shoulder. Funny, no powers. That amount of danger should have turned her to ice. I knew when I was scared, I was very hard to touch.

"How dare you!" I demanded. Redmond came up next to me, looking around at the pile of rubble that used to be my mom's house. A mean little thought came into my head. *Looked like she couldn't enjoy the money she got for me anymore.* "I was coming to protect her!"

"Drake," Mom said. "Please."

"No, Cher. This could have ruined all of us. You'd think she'd be better at this by now. Now we have to run. It's all over. They'll never believe that we got away without Gem doing something. They'll blame us. Thanks a lot, Burner." Drake was steaming.

Okay, that was it! No one told me how to do my job. This idiot was a stranger, an outsider who was just an extra in this. He had no right to lecture me.

"Look!" I screamed and turned him around. I jumped backward, grabbing Redmond.

Drake had purple eyes! Drake was a Breather.

"Oh," Mom said and looked back and forth between us. "Your contacts burned."

Drake nodded. "I got the brunt of the attack."

"You're a freaking Breather!" I screamed. "Mom, he's... You knew?"

Mom nodded. "He's my husband. Gem's father. He's also the one who helped me find out more about this world. Your world."

I slammed my fingers into fists. It hurt. Like I was trying to break them. This went beyond betrayal. I reached out for anything I could use. Water...Ah, no water pipes. Drake was smart. He knew about Burners. No wonder there was nothing for an attack.

I threw my hand out anyway, and...What the hell?

Lightning shot out of my fingers and zipped toward Drake. He nimbly, even with Gem in his arms, did a backflip in the air and dodged my...freaking lightning bolt!

"Um, Laoni? What is going on?" Redmond sounded lost, dazed and confused. Almost as much as I was. But I was angry. Mom had sold me out and then joined the very enemy who had tried to kill me.

"Don't!" Mom yelled. "Please, Laoni, you don't understand. I love him. He loves me. He's not like the others."

"Really?" I asked. I brought up my ice and slammed it into him. He drew it in, closing his eyes. The same ecstasy apparent. "That's a Breather. That's a Bloodhound."

"It's a long story," Drake said. He was still angry, but he understood me. He knew. And so did I.

"I don't want to hear it. You follow me, you're dead," I spat. I turned around on my feet and slammed my way back to the bus.

I heard Drake's voice coming after me. "I wouldn't. I don't do that! Please understand."

Redmond followed me. He slipped into the bus, started it

up, and then dodged pieces of burnt tree. The yard looked like a warzone. I had expected answers. Or if I didn't get them, maybe I could have protected my sister.

But now...

"So, that may explain why your sister doesn't have powers," Redmond said, trying to get his bearings. He was freaked out, but no more than I was. "She's half a Breather. Who knew that was even possible?"

I didn't. They were monsters. "I have no sister. I have no mother. I have a traitor and a Breather sister."

"No, Laoni, don't act like that. I saw your face." The bus was rumbling along now. It was getting further and further away from the miniature war that had just happened. Why was it that every time I left behind a building, it was in pieces?

"My face? What was my face doing?" I asked.

"You lit up when you saw Gem. There was a connection. You wanted to know her more. And..."

"Shut up," I said and looked out the window.

"Drake helped us. He gave us this." Redmond pulled up the gun from the space between us and put it back down. "It killed the Breathers. That's an asset. He just gave it over."

"Shut up!" I said again.

He wouldn't listen. "He's not evil. He loves your mom. And we did bring the Breathers after us. That was our fault. I sensed them from the moment we got there."

I bounced up an ice wall between us, making it cold enough to stay. Wisps of vapor slipped off it, and I could feel Redmond's heat on the other side trying to melt it down. Tough.

I was shutting down right now. I didn't need my mother. I didn't need a Breather sister. And if Drake had my scent now, I'd kill him.

My whole family was my enemy.

CHAPTER 8

*D*iary,
   I had to turn to you. I can't pour my heart out to anyone but you. Not even Mond understands. He keeps saying I should give them a chance. No, not just Mom. All of them. Even the freaking Breather who's playing Daddy to my sister. Ugh. My Breather sister. Not my sister.

I don't know how to handle this at all. Mond says that the man was on our side. The Breather. I won't use his name. I just won't. All the years on the run, staying away from precisely that kind of person.

That's not all. Mond is freaked out by the lightning I shot. What? Can't I have some skills he isn't aware of?

Right. I forgot who I was talking to. You know everything, Diary. You know I'm full of crap. I'm scared too. Never had lightning before.

When I shot that stuff across the room, I felt something. I had just been too overcome with the horror of the moment to pay much attention. I had felt that same feeling before, when I was in the machine.

Truth? Sometimes I need to throw the light on at night to make sure I'm not still in the machine. I never had much use for nightmares before. Get over it. Know it's false. But being inside that thing made me totally upset. That's too light of a word. Incomparably miserable.

The moment I threw my hand up and it came out, I recalled that feeling. Insane. I was free. I was fighting. How could I feel the same as when I was in that stinking, draining contraption?

Argh! I'm screaming on the inside. I had wanted Mom to welcome me home! Didn't have much hope, but when she took me in her arms and said she was sorry, how much she hated herself...

Had to stop. My tears were blurring the page. I hope I'm not staining this diary permanently. It had all worked out according to my plan. Except for one thing.

Mom was married to a Breather. Had his kid. After giving me up, she had searched for me and found him. What did that entail? I mean, Breathers are pure evil.

"Not like the others," Mom had said. Yeah freaking right.

Wait, someone's knocking.

~

Unbelievable! My boyfriend is incredible. He wanted to talk. He didn't think I wanted to be alone. And I don't. But I still told him to go away.

I can't accept any defense of my family. Did I just write that? They are not my family. I hate them all!

I want to grab that Drake jerk and squeeze his neck until his eyes pop out! How dare he steal my mother? How dare he create a sister I can't possibly love?

~

J just read what I wrote. I am being waaaaay too emotional. Yeah, too many vowels there. I am grown up now. I can't act like a child. Okay, I was being way—one vowel! —too emotional.

I have to tell you what happened when I got home. If you think Natalie didn't notice we were gone, you're being very silly. She noticed.

Oh, and she let us have it.

CHAPTER 9

"Irresponsible, stupid, ridiculous, and did I mention stupid?"

Mond and I sat in front of Natalie's pacing form in the sunken living room of the sunken house we lived in right now on a faded yellow couch with too many throw pillows. It turned out that only an hour after we left, Natalie wanted to take the bus to go and check on something. But, of course, it was gone.

I was still simmering about the whole thing. Every response came out angry and sharp. "I don't have to check in with you," I reminded her. "The girl was *my* sister. Furthermore, I've done really well in my life without *you*."

Natalie matched me glare for glare. She spun on her heels and walked up to me, putting her face in mine. "You chose to be a part of this team. You are. Get over it. You stole the bus."

"Already stolen!" I retorted, craning my neck to push back. "I just stole it again."

"We did, actually," Mond said, trying to soothe both sets of ruffled feathers. Mine were impossible. Natalie looked at him. "It was a birthday present. Laoni has never gotten one in her life. She needed this, Natalie."

Natalie went back to pacing. "You got the attention of the Breathers! You were almost killed. You destroyed a house. The police are all over it. And people saw the bus leaving. You were careless. Irresponsible."

"Redundant!" I said. "I will not sit here and be lectured, got me? You don't even know what it's like!"

Natalie bared her teeth at me. "Did you even care about what we need to do next? Or are you out? If so, then the door's that way. Go ahead. Just don't take the bus. You can go back to walking."

I deflated. I couldn't leave. Despite my rage about everything, I liked Natalie. I was the one who had done something incredibly stupid. Even I was beating myself up for it. "I don't wanna go. I chose this. I'm sorry." That was like pulling teeth, but my tone didn't placate Natalie.

She snapped, "Accepted! Did you find out anything useful?"

I shot a look at Redmond. He gestured to me as if to say *go ahead.*

"We found a Breather," I said. "He's my sister's dad."

Now that rubbed the glare right off Natalie's face. Her surprise almost made me laugh—if there was anything to laugh about right now. Shame was making its presence known in my heart. Anger faded, but shame lasted forever. I had almost gotten killed. I'd betrayed the person who had saved me. The only way I could make it up to her was to give her a mission debriefing.

After I explained everything that happened, Natalie was floored. "No. Impossible. He must be a very good liar. He seduced your mom. Easy. They're almost as attractive as we are. There must be something more. He has your scent?"

I nodded.

"Great. Wonderful. Such a good thing to happen. Thank you so much!" Natalie was back to acid.

"I'll kill him. My personal vengeance. What about my...I mean, Gem Boyer. Is she a threat? She's only ten."

Natalie sat down, kicking her legs out. To calm herself, she sent icy breaths throughout the room. She couldn't materialize ice like I could, but she was still a Burner. "I can't in good conscience call for the death of a child. I guess we wait. Besides, from what I heard, they will find a new location, and that will be hard to track down, especially when there is so much more to be done now." She worried her lip for a few minutes, her fingers doing the same to the pillows of the couch.

"Okay, now that's done," Mond said. "Can we talk about the other issue?"

I looked away. I knew what he was going to say.

"What?" Natalie asked, looking innocent.

"The lightning! We're Burners—ice and fire. That's it. But she shot lightning. What is it? Should we be worried?"

I waited for Natalie's answer. To my surprise, she laughed.

"Wow, after what you've seen, a little lightning gets you freaked?" Natalie asked.

Mond pursed his lips, embarrassed. "It's—" Mond was struggling. "—not natural."

Natalie stood up and placed a comforting hand on his shoulder. "No worries. Let's just forget it."

I noticed she hadn't answered him. It brought the conversation back in my mind I had once overheard when Natalie was talking to Nora. They were worried about me. Could it have been related?

"Let's focus!" Natalie snapped, ripping me away from my concentration. "Can we get on with it? Tonight, at midnight, we'll leave. We've got another mission in the next few days."

My ears perked up. Oh, yeah, now that was exactly what I needed. Action! "Midnight? Strange time."

"Day brings notice, as you well know."

Sweet, another dig in my general direction.

"Night covers all."

I nodded. I was more than ready for this. Redmond wasn't the only one worried about my lightning. It was like a hidden ache, yelling at me. I should notice it. Which was why I completely ignored it. "What's up? More info."

Natalie whistled sharp and clear, and Erin and Cindy came running into the living room seconds later. Neither of them was happy to see us.

"I want you all ready. That info you stole has given me three locations where Breathers are bred. If we destroy them, there will be no more births. No more hunting. The humans against us will be dealt a horrible blow, one I bet they'll never recover from." Natalie nodded.

A fierce longing filled my body. If this mission was successful, we'd just have to eliminate the Breathers that still lived, no new ones. No more running. No more fighting. I could go home…

Wow. Where had *that* come from? I didn't mean the island. It wasn't home. Plus, the old brownstone in New York was long gone. Maybe even the piece of garbage who I once called Daddy lived there. But who cared? I had to face it. Home was my mother. Since the facility, since the sewer, and even since the island, home was going back to her.

But that was impossible.

I straightened my shoulders and gestured to Natalie. "Done. Where and how long?"

Natalie gave me a smile. She had forgiven me. Cool. "We'll have to give up this hideout. I've gone over some maps. We're going toward Florida, specifically Lutz."

Erin's head snapped up. "Seriously? That's near my

parents' home! I've got a place we can stay. They had a pool when I was a kid. There was a huge sunroom around it. Perfect for a new base of operations."

Natalie slammed her hands down on the little coffee table, making Erin jump. "No way. No old lives." Natalie wasn't making many friends today.

Erin glowered at her. "It's not that."

Of course, we all knew it totally was.

"It can work. My family will welcome us all in. They knew, okay? They're for us."

Natalie growled again. I don't know if I just wanted to earn some points with Erin or if Natalie wasn't my favorite person right now, but I sided with Erin.

"You know, Erin is right. Why not check it out? In a big city, there won't be a lot of water-filled wonderlands where we can hide. Your old place is gone. And who in their right mind would take in six freaky beauties like us?"

Erin shot me a grateful glance.

"Plus, most Breathers won't hurt humans, so we could use them as human shields." I really didn't know when to shut up.

Erin gaped at me. So much for grateful.

"No, really, Natalie, think about it. We won't hear the end of Erin's whining if we don't go, and she'll probably be the idiot I was and run off." I grinned to show I was kidding.

But that got to Natalie. "I can*not* believe I'm agreeing with you. But…"

"Yes!" Erin screamed and started jumping up and down. "Oh, Cindy, wait until you meet my parents! They'll love you. And my older brother. My younger sister. Sheesh, she'll be about twelve now. Yes, yes, yes!"

Mond, Natalie, and I watched as Erin, the sourpuss cloud of darkness, lightened up and danced Cindy around the room.

"I blame you for this," Natalie said and turned around and walked off, but I could see her smile.

~

The road came swiftly under the tires. I didn't know when the journey would end or even how. We were going on a lot of what-ifs, and hopefully it'd end well. Erin was positive her family would still be in the house she had been taken from. Her parents owned their own three acres and had built a house on it.

But what if they had sold it? What if they didn't welcome her in?

Thanks to my stupidity, we had to keep looking over our shoulders. The bus was almost a dead giveaway. For the next ten hours, we all sat, tense, watching any other cars that joined us on the highway.

I kept recollecting the old days when it was just Mond and me, and when the Rider had come up from behind. The snow arrows I had created out of nothing. I had been pushed past my limits. But would this trip end in a welcoming place like it had at Natalie's Bed and Breakfast?

Erin had sunk into her usual pessimist ways, casting gazes outside to the flying dark scenery and back to me. I knew what she was thinking. We wouldn't have to worry as much if the Breathers didn't have the bus in their sights. If I hadn't given my scent to a Breather.

Then it happened. As it always did.

A Rider appeared behind us. I threw my head into my hands and jumped out of my seat, vaulting over the heads of Erin and Cindy.

"What kind?" Natalie asked.

"Rider!" I yelled. "Machinery. I'm making a storm." I didn't care if I fainted again. This was my fault.

"No, Oni!" Redmond said. "You have other people in here!"

I didn't listen. I raised my palms. Nothing happened. *Ice? Where are you?*

No one noticed my lack of action. Cindy took my cue and started concentrating on a storm. Hers fell with little pelts, but it did the trick.

The Rider reached up his hand to deflect the ice and went skidding.

"Faster!" I urged, next to Natalie now. I was jumping all over the little bus.

Natalie growled. "I'm pushing it as fast as it'll go. It's a bus, not a Ferrari."

"Next time we choose a getaway car, let me," I said. But there were no more Riders. We had caught the attention of only one.

I collapsed back in my seat. My shirt seemed too tight. The watch on my wrist was cutting off my circulation. I hadn't done a thing. I had just let Cindy do it. What was happening to me?

There was no other incident. The trip had ended better than I thought it would. We took an exit and followed Erin's directions to her old home. I swear, this was the happiest I'd ever seen her. Losing her family had turned her head.

Had the same happened to me? Was I the same person I'd be if I hadn't lost Mom?

"Turn here!" Erin said excitedly, hanging on the back of Natalie's seat. It led to a place that was on the outskirts of the city. The sun slipped through the area to reveal a square house with a doorway that pushed out, showing a porch in front of the main door. It was all done in tan and brown, fading into the short green grass all around. A brick driveway led to the front. A wooden sign planted in the grass said "Barclays' Residence."

Natalie boldly parked in front. She must have really trusted Erin. Or really trusted herself to get us out of there if things went south.

"How are we going to do this?" I asked. "Maybe I should look around—"

Erin interrupted me. "Hey, this is *my* house. You don't give the orders here, 'kay?"

I opened my mouth to argue but closed it just as fast. *But I always led!*

"I'll go to the front, make sure someone's home. If not, we'll just move into the pool house."

Wow, she sounded sure of herself.

She giggled. "It looks exactly the same. My roses are still flourishing. Look! I planted those with Dad. He loves flowers. My swing set is gone, though. It was a little plastic thing. It makes sense, though. They wouldn't keep a little kid's swing set. My sister's twelve now." She pushed the door open. Natalie didn't even try to stop her.

Great! When it comes to my home and family, it was hands-off! But Erin got to go in? What if there were Breathers in there, waiting for her to make contact?

"Stupid, really stupid," I muttered.

Mond reached back from the passenger seat and patted my hand. "I don't think any Breathers are here."

Yeah, only at my house. Correction, not *my* house.

We watched Erin's short ball of a ponytail swinging as she opened the screen and then knocked on the door.

It took only seconds before we heard a loud scream.

I slid the door open and ran toward Erin. I was ready. This time my ice wouldn't fail me!

But all I saw was an older woman holding onto Erin. She had a round dark face and a really short black haircut. Tan pants and a white blouse made her look tall. She wasn't trying to strangle Erin. She was hugging her. Like my mom did me.

I turned away, but her mom caught my retreating form.

"Who is this? Did you bring Erin back to me?"

"Well, yeah," I said.

Erin shot a glare at me. But she had to admit I had!

"I'm Laoni. Your name?"

"Call me Babs. Everyone else does."

Oh, goody, what a treat.

"Where is everyone?" Erin asked, back to ignoring me. "I want to see them!"

"Oh, Carolyn is at school! Your father is at work. You almost missed me heading to work, too. But I'll call in sick. Oh, and Butch is also at school." Her eyes flashed back and forth, but I wasn't sure she could see anything. Tears were rolling down her cheeks.

"Yeah, Erin, it's a school day," I reminded her. I was sounding like a snot, I knew I was. But this looked very much like Erin was going to get the homecoming I should have gotten. No Breathers as family!

"Right. Mom, I know this is sudden. But we're not alone. We're also kind of on the run."

Babs' face slackened. She was scared. As anyone should be. "Is it *them?*"

"You know about Breathers?" I demanded. I walked up to the front door and looked into her eyes. "What else are you hiding?"

Erin nudged me backward. "Shut up, Laoni! Don't mind her. She's paranoid to the core."

Now, *that* was funny. Just because Erin proved to be right most of the time didn't mean she wasn't paranoid herself. Way more than me!

Erin continued, still clutching her mom. "They tried to

get me before they kidnapped me," Erin added for my bene-fit. "You're the one who just told her their names."

I was out of my element here. I was supposed to fight. There was nothing to fight here.

"How many?" her mom asked. I guess she chose to ignore me. And I was so not important here. This was Erin's deal. Then why did I feel the urge to take over so much? Maybe because I wanted this to end badly, just like mine had. How petty!

"There's our friend, Natalie, and two others. Redmond and...Cindy."

I heard the pause. Oh, so Erin wasn't so sure how her mom would handle her relationship. That should be fun, at the very least.

I closed my eyes inwardly at that thought. I was being brutal here. I was selfish. I vowed to stop that.

"Can we take the pool house, please?" Erin asked. "We need water surrounding us, so *they* don't come."

Babs nodded. She was so completely clueless about our lives. But she rallied back. "Let's go! I wanna meet your friends."

She rushed out the front door and toward our bus. Natalie nodded and everyone got out. I had to admit, I'd be freaked out by the sheer amount of beauty in one inhuman wall. Babs didn't disappoint.

"Oh my God," she breathed. "Wow..."

"Hello, I'm Natalie," she said and walked forward, shaking her hand. "Pickled duck. Chicken livers. Washed out orange and crusty tangerine."

Everyone gaped at Natalie at that.

She gave us a grin. "Confusion helps dazed minds. I know we're hard to take in all at once. So, bullshit brings out sense."

Babs recovered. Nice. I had to remember that. Of course, I never had cause before to stop the power of my beauty.

Babs shook all our hands and then lingered on Redmond. She gave a blushing smile. "Oh, hi. Erin, is this your boyfriend? I approve."

Erin glanced at Cindy, who wiggled her eyebrows, but she didn't get a chance to respond. I certainly wasn't going to clear things up for her. Redmond looked flummoxed. He hadn't ever gotten used to dealing with people.

"Your father will want to ask him a whole lot of questions. Oh, I can't wait for him to come home."

She meant that literally because she pulled out a phone, and as we walked toward the back of the house, she called her husband and ordered him home from work. Then she called the schools and said there was an emergency and to send the other two home.

How exciting it must have been to be Erin at this time!

"Your green-eyed monster is showing," Mond whispered as he swung my hand.

I pursed my lips and pulled away. "Don't want Babs to get the right idea. I'd like to see Erin squirm out of this."

"How unflattering," Mond said in a whisper as we watched the backs of Erin and her mom, Natalie and Cindy trailing them.

"I'm ugly in some ways," I reminded.

"Jealousy isn't your best trait. But I'm so relieved."

I glared at him. "Why?"

"It's nice to know you aren't perfect. Before, I felt inadequate measuring up. But now, hey, you're human like everyone else!"

I laughed and felt a bit better. I was being jealous and mean. I took Mond's hand and brought it up for a kiss. "You're right. I'll behave."

"Not too much." Mond gave me a look, and I practically melted into his arms.

But we had reached the sunroom Erin had called a pool house. It was actually perfect. A large pond was behind the sunroom, giving us one body of water. The pool was almost against the wall, leaving a lot of room in between. There were little rooms inside, changing rooms, which gave privacy, and lots of lounge chairs made of waterproof fabric that'd provide places to sleep.

The whole place was green and blue. I was so glad we had brought swimsuits. Natalie had not approved, but she couldn't deny there might be a chance for swimming. It had been a while since I had the luxury of water surrounding me.

"Your father and siblings will be home soon," Babs announced as we all brought our suitcases into the sunroom and put them far away from the pool. "In the meantime, settle in. I'll order some food. What do you like?"

"Caviar and champagne," I said, just to be obstinate. I didn't care.

"Really?" Babs asked. Wow, she really took everything at face value.

Erin rolled her eyes at me. "No. Just get whatever will come fastest. Believe me, we'll eat anything. We're still discovering the textures and tastes of all this food."

Babs laughed and grabbed Erin around the neck. "And I won't let *you* out of my sight. Come on, help me not make a fool out of myself with ordering." Mom and daughter left, leaving us.

"So," Natalie said, "here we are. The breeding place of the Breathers is…"

I stopped her. "No! We just got here. I want to swim. And we won't go anywhere until dark anyway, right?"

Natalie judged me. I was being impossible. I just had no

idea of my place here. I clearly didn't lead, but I had a hard time following.

"Okay. Swim."

"Yes!" Cindy said. "Let's get changed."

A flurry of activity met that as she and Mond raced to the changing rooms. Natalie tapped my shoulder. "Can we talk?"

"Not right now. I need my diary."

I slunk off to the corner and ignored Natalie as I waited for my turn to change.

CHAPTER 10

A large dining room filled with people wasn't what I expected to unnerve me. But there I was, sitting around a large table, keeping my hands on my knees and my face down. I didn't know how to handle Erin's family.

They didn't seem to care much about me either. Everything was Erin. Erin's friends. Erin's teacher—they thought Natalie was some teacher at a special school. I sat next to Mond and counted down the minutes until we could get out of there.

According to Natalie, we had to play the parts of perfect guests. We didn't need them getting scared.

I lapsed into silence, and no one knew or cared. It had been strange being on my own, stranger being with people, but almost too much to bear being ignored.

"So, Erin, go on," Babs said as she handed a bowl of mashed potatoes to Erin's brother. His grin was so wide it hurt. He was so happy to have his sister back. "You were saying? After a few years in that facility, you did what?"

I stared at her. What was she going to tell them? How much of a war we had gone through?

"Not much," Erin said. She had chickened out. Probably for the best. How much would her family want to know she was some kind of warrior now? Sneaking around and breaking into places.

"And this is your boyfriend?" Ralph asked. Erin's father had been chomping at the bit to ask that question. After the preliminary joy at having her back, the lengthy conversation about her life, and then a long rendition of what happened in their own lives—Babs was a librarian; Ralph was some kind of software engineer—he finally could speak.

I guess it wasn't every day your long-lost daughter came home and brought a boy with her. Of course, they'd jump to the wrong conclusions. I think a better question would have been how long she could stay, what we were planning, and how soon, yes, would she be going into danger where she could get killed. But that's just me.

Maybe they were just idiots. Or...I sighed into my plate as I realized what they wanted to know was probably safer for them. They couldn't wrap their brains around her powers. Erin also didn't want to tell them.

This was a façade, and we were all supposed to play along.

Still, it might be fun to see Erin squirm out of every inquiry.

"If so, then, are you just young lovers? Do you have morals? Being safe? How long are you going to be together?" Ralph shot the questions off like a gun. Was that what a father was supposed to do? I wasn't sure. Mine had been a very bad example.

I stared at Erin as she looked at her father. "Dad, stop. Please. Redmond is *not* my boyfriend. No. Cindy is my girlfriend."

A silent bomb hit the room. Wonderful! She came back out of the blue, after having been kidnapped when she was little, and she has the ability to control fire, and the thing that stymied them all was who her girlfriend was? As funny as it was, these people needed to rethink their priorities.

"Oh," Ralph said.

"That's, um, wonderful," Babs said.

Ralph looked back and forth between the two, nodded, and spoke. "Okay, then, Cindy. Are you just young lovers? Do you have morals? Are you being safe? And how long are you going to be together? Because no one, and I mean no one, will break my little girl's heart, got me?"

Everyone started talking at once. Back on their explosion of words and greetings. I pushed my chair out slowly and slipped out, unnoticed.

I wasn't hoping for anything bad. But did they all have to be so…loving? I hated them all in that moment. Not because they were bad. They were good. They were right. Accepting Erin for who she was.

But it made me feel like a mean and cold little miser in my heart. Something was wrong. Like, maybe I should have asked a few more questions when I found out Drake was a Breather. Everything in me said, no way! If I saw any of them again, I'd kill them.

But I didn't know. Mom had yelled, "He's not like the others." She loved him. Love! How could it be wrong?

It just was. My mind shrunk, and I ran back out to the pool house. I pushed my fist into my mouth and started to cry. I had had the same homecoming! But it had been me who had judged and ran away, not my mom.

"Two arms, no waiting," Mond said, slipping up behind me. Of course! He would notice I'd left. My heart jumped just a bit. He was my world. I needed him so much. I took his offer and let him wrap his big strong arms around me. He kissed my head and murmured platitudes again and again. I melted into his embrace.

Finally, he tilted my face up and gave me a kiss. "What is it? This welcoming is hard for you. Because you didn't get the same?"

I knew he'd understand. But I just couldn't form the words. "Oh, Mond. I hate myself right now. I should be happy for her. I wanted her family to turn on her. Kick her out. What does that say about me?"

"It says you're a person who has been wounded, and sometimes you want to turn that wound on others. But it was all inside. You can't hate yourself for thoughts. Just deeds. You did nothing to hurt Erin or her family. You've been a perfect guest. Disappearing when you needed to."

I felt myself relax in his arms. My cheek hit his and I pushed into it, trying to feel his warmth.

"Ouch!" he yelled. "Do you have sharp ice on your cheek or something?"

I pulled away and looked at his face. It was red! "What in the?" I asked.

Mond rubbed his cheek. "What's happening to you?" he asked. Worry filled his tone. "Your ice is out of control. You're…"

I stiffened and stood up. "Go on, Redmond. Tell me what's happening. I don't know."

"You're burning me. I know the situation. I did it to my girlfriend before she broke up with me."

I cocked my head. "You never told me that last part."

His shoulders reached his ears. He looked more miserable than I had ever seen him. "Hey, people leave me. I told you that. But I'm…Would I seem weak if I told you I'm terrified out of my skin right now?"

"Of me?" I asked. I walked the long side of the pool and slid into one of the chairs. Mond followed. As stupid as he was being, he slid next to me and cocooned my body with his.

"No, not of you. A dangerous touch is just as good as a nice one. But of something that is wrong. You're getting worse. Did you notice it? I should have known this relationship was too perfect. My life was too good."

I rolled over face to face with him, wanting desperately to cuddle him to me. But I had seen what happened. Something really was wrong. "Ah, my friend the pessimist is back."

"Never left." He sighed and stroked my chin, carefully, like he was stroking fire. I held my breath. It took only seconds before he pulled away. "This is impossible! The one thing that's worked from the beginning was us."

I should have told him. Nothing ever lasted long with me. No home. No friends. No family.

"Mond, we need to know what's wrong…"

We were interrupted by our friends coming back from dinner. Cindy was laughing and poking Erin.

"I've never seen you blush so much," she teased.

"Yeah, what about you and your intentions? Should have told you, my father wants to go back in time a hundred years."

"Nope, he's quite modern," Cindy returned. They looked to where we were and blinked.

"Oh, I guess I forgot about you two," Erin said. "Sorry. It's just…"

"You family loves you. Never apologize for that. It's good," I said. Mond and I stood up.

"What happened to you?" Erin asked alarmed. The wound was still apparent on his face. "Did someone attack?"

Mond shook his head. "I cut myself shaving. No biggie." He turned away and busied himself somewhere in the corner.

Natalie strolled in and looked toward us. Without a word, she started unpacking some blankets. "We need some sleep, kiddos. We haven't slept since last night. We're all tired."

I caught a blanket tossed to me. "Never call me kiddo," I said and chose my bed. I stared off into the darkening gloom outside. My mind was worried

"Keep ready. We're going at midnight again," Natalie warned.

"Only a few hours of sleep?" Cindy groaned. "Oh, this is just perfect." But she shut up before Natalie could chew her head off. "Your family's nice," I heard her tell Erin.

I closed my eyes. I couldn't help it. I saw no future anymore. Every minute of every day, I was back in that machine, stuck there, being drained. I couldn't think or feel without remembering that. Mond had gotten hurt. My powers, which had been so reliable, were leaving me.

Somehow, I felt Mond's hand reaching for me. A comforting whisper hit my ears. "We'll handle it together. There is nothing to worry about. We'll always be together. Even if you burn me forever."

I smiled. I fell asleep with the comfort of his hand around mine. No burning.

Maybe it had been a fluke. Maybe it was just when I was upset I hurt him.

My dreams held me in the machine. Lightning convulsed my entire body and ran rampant, obliterating my ice. Destroying anything I was.

When Natalie woke me up, I looked over Mond's hand. It was blistered and raw.

"Natalie!" I shrieked.

She rushed over and started looking at it. Her face tightened. "Mond, can you fight?"

"Easy," he said, grimacing. "It's just one hand. Totally worth it." He said it for my benefit. But I couldn't feel.

I was beyond thankful that there was a mission. Natalie

did some first aid on Redmond's hand and bandaged it up. A slice of despair hit every single time I looked at the bandage. Erin and Cindy were confused. They had woken up to my shriek and stood quietly by while Natalie did her first aid stuff. They had no clue on what was going wrong with Redmond.

I knew. It was me. I had hurt him.

Natalie didn't say anything except to give us the basics. The night was dark behind the pool house. Everything was so unearthly still, it almost felt as if I was still dreaming.

"We get in, explode everything in sight. Nothing is spared. Try to find La Madre," Natalie ordered.

I put all my fears and worries into what was happening next. It's what I did best. Survive through danger, not cry in the night wondering when I'd hurt my world again. "Who is La Madre?"

"I'm not sure. According to the notes, it's something that helps the Breathers get born. Created. I don't know. It's a fenced-in facility. I'll pull around to the back."

Part of my brain heard what we had to do, but the rest was spinning like a top. What exactly was I going to find in there? I had never really thought about the origin of the Breathers. I was beyond grateful to find out that they were unnatural creations. But were we going to walk into Frankenstein's lab or what?

CHAPTER 11

*W*e hit the ground running. This was a lot different from the quiet, info-gathering we had done on the last mission. This was hit-and-run—heavy cannon tactics.

I brought the gun that the Breather had given me. It was an amazing piece of technology. Some kind of recharging beam that obliterated anything it touched. The only downside was that it took time to recharge after a few shots. Where Drake had gotten it, and how, didn't matter.

I banged out the beams and ran forward. Again, there were no human guards. A relief to me. I didn't want to be a murderer of their kind. I was here for the evil.

They attacked.

Two Breathers came in from the left as we bashed down the gates with an icy battering ram. I wish I could say that was me. Cindy had been practicing. Redmond and Erin were hands-on. Any Breather could absorb their powers, but a punch couldn't be absorbed.

The place was packed with Breathers! They were around

every corner. We worked back-to-back, inching our way to the front.

I zipped my gun through the night. When the Breathers realized what we could do, they showed their cowardice and ran. Good enough! It let us keep moving forward.

The huge area outside the one-story, white-and-black building was all concrete. No forest here, of course. There were no Burners here. The forest didn't protect Breathers, so why be bothered by nature? Instead, the place was completely surrounded by a seven-foot stone fence. As usual with these places, it wasn't within city limits. It existed halfway down a highway, far back from the road. A narrow lane led us in.

"Behind you!" Redmond yelled. I turned and fired. A particularly lovely Breather dodged and grabbed me.

"Die, Burner!" he hissed. I tried to throw him off with my ice. But the traitor didn't show its face.

I slammed my elbow in and fired again. Caught him in the chest. He just collapsed and I scurried out from under him. I nodded my thanks to Redmond.

I fired again. But nothing came. Needed a recharge.

I pulled the old throw-an-empty-weapon-at-the-enemy thing and caught the next Breather on the head—followed by an explosion. The Breather was caught in the face and fell. The others were running.

"Thanks, Redmond!" I yelled. I reached down and picked up the gun. I didn't want to lose it. To my amazement, it still functioned even after Redmond's burst of fire.

"Almost there," Erin said. "Let's keep the gratitude to when we're finished. There are more inside. They want to protect this place."

I rolled my eyes. Like I didn't know that!

"Why can't we just psshh!" Redmond asked, gesturing with his fire to the building.

Natalie fielded that one. "We might miss one," her voice crackled. "We need to make sure every single thing is gone.

"Erin, follow me. Cindy, Redmond, head toward the other side. We'll come in like a pincer and squeeze them between us. Once inside, we'll have a lot more ammo. Go."

Erin listened without hesitation. That made me smile inside. Outside, I was already throwing a metal door open after Erin burned the hinges. I was their leader.

Even Erin's.

"Okay, there will be six hallways with rooms down each," Natalie's voice said in my earpiece. "Those rooms will have Breathers being born and raised. But there's a main computer you have to destroy as well."

"That's me," Redmond's voice said inside my ear. I heard him grunt. He must have been fighting.

The hallways were lit with ball lights in concaves at the top every six feet or so. It made it look like the interior of some alien spaceship. Whoever built this was a little nuts. There was one main hallway that led to smaller ones to the right and left, which ended in doors. Straight through, I saw one large opening with double doors. The floor beneath my feet was concrete. No embellishments. It was a cold world.

"Split up," I told Erin as I saw Cindy and Redmond breaking off from each other as well. "Destroy every single Breather."

"Will they be…" Cindy. She sounded hesitant. I saw her freeze far off in front of me. She cast a look at both of us. "Are they babies?"

I didn't like that idea at all. But even if they were…They couldn't truly be innocent, could they? My sister flashed into my mind. I hesitated.

Erin didn't. "Kill them or they will grow to kill us."

I nodded and rushed to the left hallway. I needed my cold, mission-mind, but it was abandoning me. What were we doing here? Breaking into a nursery to kill babies? Were they as evil then? Did they learn their morals or were they darkness incarnate?

"Status," Natalie barked in my ears. "You should be inside by now. What do you see?"

"I…"

"Laoni, they're Breathers. Get going," Erin said. I cast a look down the hallway to see Erin looking at me from far off.

I listened to her orders. Some leader.

But I couldn't rely on my mind. I was scared. What was I becoming?

I slammed the door open. Breathers attacked. I couldn't see behind them. These Breathers were wearing lab coats. I used my fists, spinning over their heads to pull them down best as I could.

Then a beep hit my hip. Ah, my weapon was recharged. I really loved that thing!

Hmm, given to me by the same thing I was killing with it.

I shook my head and filled the room with light. Bodies fell, and I could see…

"Holy…" Cindy. She had seen something. "Do you see this?"

I was relieved she was okay. I hated splitting up. But we only had so many people. It was a good thing they hadn't expected a surprise attack. Natalie was good.

I looked around, the battle lust fleeing from my eyes.

Well, Cindy was shocked. I was horrified. A few expletives filled my ears as the rest of my team saw what we had come for.

Thank whatever, they *weren't* babies.

Fully grown monsters of slime and bone, that's what. Or at least what I could see from the top half.

What the other Breathers were guarding looked like large

open wombs. Round in shape and placed on stick-like pedestals. There were at least a dozen in there. Half of them were encased in a pouch full of bubbling goo. Their nude tops were surrounded by more goop and connected to thousands of tubes. Every orifice was connected to a cylinder, which went from every womb here to a major channel overhead filled with…I don't know. It was a slimy yellow. I had a feeling that if I killed them, they'd explode into that goo.

Their purple eyes were blank, unseeing. Their chins stuck to their chests, and their hands were clasped across their chests like they were placed to die. Flashing lights were on each womb, going from yellow to green.

Only one was a bright green, and that one had fewer tubes attached. It was almost ready.

"What do we do?" Cindy asked. "Just, um, stab them? Step on them like cockroaches?"

I gritted my teeth. "Pull the plug." I grabbed hold of one of the tubes and yanked. It came loose easily and sprayed yellow gunk everywhere. I dodged it and yanked on another. And another.

"This is so utterly gross," Cindy complained.

I had to agree, but infinitely preferable to killing babies. These Breathers were truly monsters.

"People, on your toes!" Redmond warned. "The computer is angry."

I hurried up, but it was too late. I was only two-thirds through when the Breathers' eyes opened.

"Well, now," one said. "I didn't realize I would have so much fun when we first came to. You're so pretty. Let me hold you."

I fired my gun, but to my surprise, he jumped over the beam and landed next to me.

"So pretty," he said and grabbed my shoulders.

"I've got problems!" Erin yelled. "Backup? Please."

I tried to wiggle out of the Breather's hands, but more were coming, pulling their own tubes out. Intent on killing me. Some were dying on the floor. Not ready. Others were weeping from every orifice, but they were still coming for me.

The Breather that held me leaned in and licked my cheek. "Tasty!" he said.

I slammed my elbow into his gut and fired again and again. But I had heard Erin's cries.

Finally, my battle-ready mode turned on. All it took was a whole lot of disgusting Breathers, but I was on again. I slammed through the door, skidding a bit on all the disgusting whatever on the floor. I ran around the corner to where Erin had gone in.

I slammed the door open. I wasn't the only one who had heard her cries for help. Cindy was already here, yanking the goop into frozen blades and slamming through the newly born Breathers' bodies.

But there were so many in here. I fired as fast as I could.

The door broke off its hinges as Redmond burned in behind us. "Ah, the situation's covered. Great! We need to get out of here."

"What's going on?" I asked.

"La Madre. A supercomputer. It started a self-destruct sequence."

"For a building?" I asked. "That's so...cool." I had to admit.

"Cool or not, it's nuclear. It's going to destroy everything here, even the Breathers." Redmond sent some fiery ceiling onto the head of a Breather who was coming close. "It was the only choice. It's a failsafe. Just in case they lost control over the Breathers."

"How do you know?"

Redmond sighed. "A human was in charge of the supercomputer. She's in love with me now. So, I sent her out of here."

"Oh, the charming Burner," I teased. But I wasn't much in the mood. The almost alive Breathers were hissing and trying to get back together.

They were pushing against each other. And…

"Oh, gross!" Cindy yelled. I agreed.

The Breathers were…joining. The goop surrounding them was some kind of uniter. A shoulder pushed against another shoulder, and one Breather was sucked into the other.

"Not babies," I told Cindy.

She agreed. "Just monsters. Good, let's get out of here. Let them explode by themselves."

Another Breather was shwooped into a neck. It was growing.

"Can all of them do this?" I asked. This went beyond my understanding of these things.

"Get out of there," Natalie insisted. "We've got company outside. Meet me on the west side, I'm…" Explosions sounded, and the mic cut off.

"No!" I yelled. "Go."

As we turned around, though, the open door met our gaze with a whole lot of Breathers lined up and ready to kill.

"Oh, how nice," one said and stepped forward. I recognized him.

So did Erin. "Paul?" she asked.

"You've caused some trouble here. A whole lot of dead Breathers. Hmm, more for me. I didn't think I'd see any of you again. I had been so looking forward to draining you," he added to Erin.

"What is this?" I demanded, stepping forward. The gloppy goop of Breathers kept growing. The smell of mold mixed with old socks filled the room.

"I believe it's what you call a trap. We have people watching every breeding ground. She knew Natalie wouldn't be able to resist destroying us at our source."

That was confusing, to say the least. "Who?"

"Our creator. Now, come quietly, or we can and will kill all of you. Be nice, and maybe we'll talk."

I'd heard that before.

An explosion suddenly rocked the building.

Paul's eyes widened. "What was that?"

Redmond grinned and stood next to me. "Self-destruct. Wanna stay and play or run and fight another day?"

Paul closed his eyes and clenched his fists. "Both. Get them!"

Then the coward pushed past the other Breathers and ran as fast as he could.

We were trapped by newborn Breathers who were melding into something bigger and by a bunch of Breathers who didn't seem to have the same self-preservation skills as Paul did. Oh, and by an explosion that was even now eating the building bit by bit.

CHAPTER 12

I have been hunted, trapped, captured, and even tortured. Nothing was quite the same as being in that room full of Breathers in front of me and constantly melding Breathers behind me, filling the area with the most disgusting sound I had ever heard.

Shwoop.

Shwoop.

Shwoop.

And in front of us were more evil Breathers, the sound of rubble intensifying.

Redmond tapped, tapped, tapped with his fire, aiming at the ceiling, bringing the overhead sprinkler system down in a twisted form of fire and melted metal. It burst into pieces. Shrapnel tore through the forces in front. The others were still melding, growing.

Cindy and Erin alternated between ice and fire attacks. They worked in unison to freeze and fry.

But there was just not enough time. My gun was useless. We backed up. The very ground underneath us rumbled. Pressure built like I had never felt before.

We were all going to die. The Breathers, the disgusting and the evil. My friends. Mond.

Strange, I usually thought of him in his full name when we went into battle. But this time, I called out to him. This wasn't going to end well. Never could.

My ice was non-existent. Maybe I could have done something more before, but now, I just felt energy slipping through my body. Screaming. My heart wanted to explode. I couldn't function. As the explosion reached the interior, I looked into Mond's eyes.

"No, not this time," I said, almost in an awed voice.

Electricity coursed through me. At first, I thought it was the explosion ripping my skin off. But no.

One minute, there was a building around me, the next, a bus. I was behind Natalie, Mond was in the front seat, and Erin and Cindy were behind me.

A mushroom cloud exploded behind us.

I wondered how they'd cover this up. Nuclear explosions don't just get swept under the rug.

Natalie jumped a mile. She hit her head on the ceiling.

"What the…!" she screamed. But she had the presence of mind to keep driving. Once again, I vaulted over the seats to stare out the back, hoping to catch our tails. The metal around the bus was crackling. I grabbed the power without thinking and tossed it backward, ripping the Breathers off the road.

Two more.

Natalie slammed onto the highway and sped through the night.

I collapsed in the back. My eyes closed on their own accord, but I wasn't sleeping. Unlike last time, I wasn't drained. I was livid with energy. Like a hundred jolts of energy were making me move. I couldn't sleep.

"What happened?" Natalie asked, speeding back toward Erin's place.

"Laoni! She transported us," Cindy answered. "Not with ice. Not with fire. But with pure lightning. We almost exploded!"

I didn't open my eyes to stare at her. I knew something was wrong with me. My hair was standing on end, charged with energy, just like my skin. I kept my hands on my head, rocking.

"Oni?" Mond asked.

Natalie stopped him. "Don't touch her. She could be dangerous."

I knew that. I was now. More than ever. If Mond touched me, he'd be burned.

"What am I?" I demanded. "Natalie, what do you know?"

"Don't worry about it tonight. We need rest. You did a good job. Nothing could have survived that explosion." She drove on. The dark streets behind us slipped under the tires. The glass of the bus windows reflected me. Lightning surrounded me. No ice.

I was no longer a Burner.

But what the hell was I?

But something about what Natalie said stayed with me. Nothing could have survived that explosion. Somehow, I didn't think so. Maybe because when I turned us all into pure energy, I felt the explosion go through us all. It ripped through the Breathers—all of them.

I saw the ones attacking us crumbling into dust. Slipping away like ash in the wind.

But the others? They didn't move. They just kept uniting, making a bigger form. Becoming new. They hadn't died.

They had been born.

CHAPTER 13

*D*iary,

    I can't sleep. I thought I would be able to. That had been close. The closest I have ever been to death. And I was going to watch my true love and my friends die at the same time. I don't even know what happened. One minute I was terrified. Then, it was like someone flipped on a switch. I turned on. I saved them all.

Natalie took me aside after everyone went to bed. She nodded toward the far end of the pool. We sat, and she stared at me.

I started the conversation. "You know." That was simple enough. Oh, Diary, I wanted to say, "Tell me, damn it. You dared to keep a secret about me?" But I was trying to be polite. The woman did save us after all. How can I hate someone who risked her own safety going after the ones that were born different?

I kept my anger to a minimum. Luckily by then, my lightning had faded away, so when Natalie took my hand and held it, I didn't kill her.

"Laoni," she said. Diary, her voice sounded so...I can't even describe it here. It was terrified or awed. Or angry. Maybe all of it. "You were in the machine and didn't die. That has never happened."

I knew when she said never that it was a lie. It had happened. "When?" I asked her. I hated begging. But I was. I wanted to know what was happening. Mond had already fallen asleep. I wanted to go and curl up by his side. But I'm not sure I can ever do that again.

That thought terrifies me more than the Breathers.

"Only in rumors. Look, the Burners haven't been around all that long—fifty, sixty years, maybe. I'm not really sure. No one knows what they are or where they came from. When Nora and I were young, our abilities started manifesting, and no Breathers came after us."

Now, Diary, can you blame me for being stunned by that? I just thought the two of them had the same trials as we all did. In fact, I never thought about the beginning of the Burners. Not really. Now, though, if we weren't a part of nature before, what are we now? A mutation? An aberration? What?

Natalie didn't know.

"Our parents were hard-pressed finding help for us. But there were others. Mama and Papa scoured the world for signs of others. We found them. Then the Breathers came."

I didn't ask. I wanted to. But Natalie was tired. There was more here than either of us knew. I just stuck to the facts.

"When we were eighteen," Natalie continued, "the machine showed up. Our kind was kidnapped and put into it. They died. The energy was sold, or so I'd imagine. It powered so many different businesses, but I think mainly it was used to create more machines and places that someone could put us. There was..."

I hate this, Diary! Natalie was crying. She hadn't thought about this stuff in many years, and I was bringing it all back. According to Natalie, there was a guy she knew. A lover, I was guessing, because there was a certain shade on her face as she talked about him.

He had survived the machine.

But he's dead now. Are you surprised, Diary? His own light-

ning ate him from the inside out. He hurt Natalie. She called him an Alternate Burner. Something that doesn't live happily inside the skin, but burns anything it touches, even the bearer's own body. Breathers aren't immune. Nothing is.

Yep, that's me now—an Alternate Burner.

How did I handle that, Diary? I turned off. I went back to business. Hey, if I have a ticking time bomb in me, I have to leave a legacy. Are you wondering why I'm okay with this?

Because, duh, Diary! I never thought I'd live long. I have seen so much death. When that happens to someone, it's only natural to wonder when they'll go away permanently.

So, I switched gears. I didn't even ask how long I had. I don't think Natalie knew anyway. I asked about other stuff.

Specifically, "She."

When I told Natalie that the person behind the Breathers, the creator, knew her name personally, that was a shock to her. She didn't know who it could possibly be, but she put it on the long list of other things she didn't know.

We're heading out again to another Breather breeding ground tomorrow.

I only asked one more question.

Can Breathers, new ones...Oh, sheesh, I need a name. Okay, Neo Breathers, can they survive a nuclear explosion?

I wasn't surprised to hear that Natalie had no clue. She thinks they're dead. I'm not so sure. In fact...I'm kinda positive, Diary. They're out there. I just know it.

So, I have to get in touch with my new deadly powers. Mond is asleep, and I can't touch him. Nothing much else to do tonight. Because when I hit the next gross set of artificial wombs, I'm going in blazing. I will not let them become another one of those disgusting creatures.

I need to spill this somewhere. I might sound blasé about dying, about this energy, but I'm not. I'll be leaving Mond behind. I'll hurt him. I'm racking my brain trying to figure out a way to make it easier on him.

I have no clue how. I'm crying. I'm not crying tears. I had just gotten used to the tickle of real water, but it's gone now. Like all my liquid has dried up.

My lightning is changing me.

I can't sleep. I can't cry. And I'm trying to figure out how to break up with my boyfriend.

What, do I live under a curse or something? Because clearly, whoever made me hates me. Who did make us? Were we all born in a lab somewhere and sent to parents by the stork?

My mind is silly tonight. But I wonder about our origins. Natalie doesn't know. She doesn't even know who the creator is.

She gave me a look. "That's the next mission, after we end the Breathers' chances. Plus..."

She was hesitant to tell me. But she did. Guess it's because she knows I'm dying. Why not tell me everything I need to know?

This gets even weirder. Turns out, the info we stole says that the energy stolen from Burners isn't only sold for lots of money. Part of it is diverted. To what? According to Natalie, it's to power something called the Better Suit. Sounds like something you'd wear to a wedding.

But if that many Burners' energy has gone into it, it's loaded with energy. But for what? Who's wearing it? And who is "she?" Only time will tell.

I think Natalie wants me to find out soon. She hinted at a recon mission but hasn't let anyone else know about it. It's going to be me. And you know why?

Because I'm the only one who can go on a suicide mission and not really risk anything!

Wheee. My life just keeps getting better and better. Now, if you don't mind, I'm going to throw my freaking pencil against the pool house wall and cry tearless tears. Hope you don't mind!

CHAPTER 14

$\mathcal{I}$ sat in the bathroom, reveling in my seclusion. The Barclays had welcomed us in, and right now, it gave me what I needed most—a place away from Redmond. He had been looking at me all morning, giving me not-so-subtle hints to go be alone with him.

I had disappeared. I wasn't being stupid. The Breather could easily find me without a ton of water around me, but I had to believe the water in this particular room masked my scent.

I didn't do much but stare and try not to think of the future, which was really hard to do when I had nothing else on my mind.

Babs was getting ready for work. We had only been here a couple of days, but were going to leave as soon as Natalie consulted with Nora. Natalie wanted to know if we had to lie low or could leave, what the story was on the nuclear explosion and all that stuff.

But Babs was acting like we were here to stay. I heard her planning a shopping trip with Erin and her sister.

I just sat there, feeling the buzzing. Before, I had felt the water, like an old friend on the edge of my mind. But now, all I felt was energy.

"Oh, hi, Redmond, wasn't it?" Babs' voice carried through the house.

"Yeah." His tones rippled through my bones. He was confused. I couldn't help him with that. "I was just wondering. Have you seen Laoni? She isn't in the pool house. So, I thought…"

Babs knew exactly where I was. But, bless her heart, she answered, "Nope. Maybe she went on a mission. I think Butch wanted to get some snacks. She might have gone with him."

I heard the pain in his voice when he answered. "Really? Did she say anything? Leave any kind of message for me?"

Babs laughed loudly. "Now, come on. It's not the end of the world for the girl to leave you alone for a few minutes. Come on, I'll make you some chocolate milk and cookies."

I wasn't at all surprised when Redmond snarled at her. "No, thank you. I'll just go and wait for her back. If she comes back here first, let her know I'm looking for her."

"Will do!" Babs chirped.

Then his heavy footsteps turned to leave. Funny, I think he paused right outside where I was, like he could sense me. I held my breath, waiting. But he continued on.

A second later, I heard a knock, and Babs entered. "Hey, he seems nice."

I gave a false grin. "He is. But I have no choice."

Babs stared at me, closing the door behind her. She slid onto the side of the tub next to me, letting her feet move the little pink bathmat around. "Do you really have no choice? Is it your abilities?"

Wow, she had no clue about how deep this danger went. "Basically. You do know Erin won't stay." I decided to lay it all out there. Besides, this kept her confused and sad eyes away from a subject I *really* didn't want to discuss. "She's in this. I think we'll leave soon, and we won't tell you where we're going."

Babs nodded. She ran her fingers through her hair. It had six barrettes in it, all shaped like multi-colored butterflies, giving a nice contrast to her hair. "I know. It's hard. She just came back. I waited for this day. I dreamed of it. I've been given my fondest wish. It's not so bad, having to let your baby go when you've gotten that, right?"

Maybe she was right. I had such a great time with Mond. I shouldn't be mourning it so much already. But I didn't want to lose it. It wasn't fair! To stop *that* four-year-old's response, I quickly flipped the toilet paper roll and changed the subject. "She's going to go into danger." I wondered if Erin had told her mom that yet.

Babs clenched her fists. "I understand. Look, a parent has worries. Lots and lots of worries. The normal stuff, what happens if my child is abducted, what if the child dies, and so on and so forth. But the worst has already happened, and she's still here. My other worry was a longstanding one, one I'd grow old with. The wonder about if your child will choose a dangerous career. Cop, army, things like that. Truth is, even without your…world, a child can grow up to get involved in a career that puts them in danger. It was always a possibility. But…Erin came back once. She'll find her way home again. I believe that."

Wow…Babs sounded so convincing. But there was something in her eyes. She didn't really believe it. It was a good thing that Erin never was in that machine. Only I was. I was the one with a death knell.

"You ready to come out? Let that poor miserable boy off the hook?" She winked one of her shiny eyes at me.

I shook my head. "If you don't mind, I want to stay here.

Natalie knows where I am, and she will come and get me when it's time. You just don't understand."

Babs sighed. "Maybe I don't." She stood up, touched my shoulder briefly, and then left. Only a minute later, she came back and put a tablet at my feet, along with some books and cookies. "Enjoy."

I almost smiled. I touched the tablet.

Oh, and fried it. It was gone. Poor Babs!

I picked up the books. They had a better ending. I don't know if paper wasn't bothered by my electricity or what, but I could read. Babs' selection was silly. A horror novel. Pass. I went through danger on a regular basis. Why would I want my heart pounding for fun?

I did, however, find the romance novels promising. Happy endings. The couples always made it out together.

I sat there in the bathroom, reading. Ignoring my brain. Wondering what if.

Redmond didn't leave me alone. For the rest of the day, he popped into the main house and bugged every single family member there.

"Have you seen Laoni?" he asked Ralph. Since Babs caught her husband as soon as he got home and made sure he knew my bathroom was off limits, he didn't tell Mond.

"Maybe she's in the pool house. You want to watch this show with me? It always keeps you guessing!"

Mond groused and left again. He came back like an hour later, when Butch was home. Butch, luckily, knew the cover story.

"Oh! Yeah, I think she went somewhere by bus. She'll be back soon." Then Butch ran away.

None of them were very good at lying, minus Babs, so I think Redmond saw right through them. But what could he do? It wasn't his house.

I could feel his desperation growing, and every single

time I heard his voice, the words on the page of the book I was reading blurred together and I grew short of breath. That hurt—far more than I thought it would!

I had decided it'd be easier to just avoid him. He'd get the point. If I could just do it long enough, maybe he'd go back to the island on one of the next runs and he'd be free. There'd be plenty of girls who'd want him.

Funny. I wanted to personally wrestle any Burner who thought they could take him from me.

I'm doing this for him, I told myself. I didn't want him to watch me die. I didn't even want him to know.

There was a knock at the door.

"What?" I asked.

Natalie opened it up. "Hey, Laoni. We've got problems. Come on. I'll give everyone the same debriefing."

I sighed and let the book fall to the floor. The happy ending had been interrupted. Much like the one Redmond and I were supposed to have.

The night was shining with stars as we walked out the door, heading toward the pool house. Everyone was inside, and I could see Redmond sitting on one of the loungers, tossing little balls of fire into the pool, watching them steam away.

"He's been going off the wall," Natalie said. "I think—"

Oh, goody. Someone else weighing in on what I should do.

"—you're doing the right thing," she said, surprising me. "I watched Stuart die. Every single day—" She choked up, seeing something far off. "—I see his body giving up. Just falling apart. When I close my eyes at night. When I blink too long. I wouldn't have had it any other way. But I could have been spared."

"You would have preferred to always wonder what had happened to him?"

Natalie gripped her hands together, squeezing her nails

one by one. "Maybe. It might have been better. But if it were me, I'd make sure to keep my loved ones away from pain. You are a selfless person, Laoni. I'm proud to have…"

Her voice broke, and she hurried away. Great. She cared for me, too. And I was doing the same thing Stuart had. Maybe I'd save Redmond, but I wouldn't save the rest.

I had to try and get away. To be on my own again. After the missions were complete. After we found out who "she" was and destroyed any chance of the Breathers coming back.

I followed Natalie into the pool house and saw Redmond's eyes light up. He rushed over to me and tried to hug me. I disappeared behind Natalie, like I had planned on being on the opposite side the whole time.

"Where were you? Did you enjoy spending the day with Butch?" Redmond crossed his arms over his chest. He'd gotten my not-so-hidden slight. If names were weapons, Butch's would have been a very sharp and bloody dagger. Mond thought that I had spent the day with another guy.

I looked at him. I swallowed my pain. I wanted to reassure him. Instead, I drove the dagger in. "Butch is very nice."

Erin's eyes rounded. "You and my brother, seriously?"

"Whoa! Did *not* see that coming," Cindy decided to weigh in.

"Okay, people!" Natalie clapped her hands together for attention. "Though the dating habits of your friends might be very interesting to normal teenagers, you are far from normal. I have news."

That stopped everything. I wanted to die right then and there as Redmond looked at me, but even he got down to business.

"Nora sent me a message. It turns out, they covered up the nuclear explosion as a gas fire. They have blocked off the streets leading toward the remnants of the building. No one knows about it."

I gaped. They got away with that?

"People believe what they're told," Natalie said to my gaping mouth. "The problem is the Breathers, the ones that joined together."

"Neo Breathers," I offered. Everyone stared at me. "That's what I call them."

"They're not so easy to contain. They didn't die in the explosion."

I closed my eyes and almost fell into the pool. Natalie steadied me. Good thing, too, because Redmond was on his way to. I couldn't take his touch right now. I would have fallen into his arms just like the pool. But I'd probably burn him.

"They're slipping around at night in the city, killing anything they touch and…absorbing them."

I shook my head. "What? They're what?"

"The Neo Breathers, as you dubbed them," Natalie said, "are intelligent. They know that if they attack in the day, there might be a possibility they'll be stopped. Every Breather is born with a full set of mental faculties. Danger-ous, and highly…malleable. As they suck in new members, they grow in size and strength. Nora and I agreed that we'd need some backup for these monsters. She sent some out on the next sub, but it'll take a few days to get here. I don't want the chance of this Neo Breather taking any Burner into it. That would supply a firepower that would be unstoppable. That means we don't all go."

"No, I will," I said quickly. "My new powers can obliterate them. And I highly doubt they'd suck me in."

Natalie nodded. "If you can't destroy them, then just hold them off until Nora's team can get here. She's got an idea of how to stop it."

"I'll go with her!" Redmond said.

"I'm going alone. Right, Natalie?" I said, begging her to agree.

She nodded. "Yes. Face it, Redmond, you could get sucked in. This Neo Breather has the same abilities as normal ones. Same skills. And since there's probably a Bloodhound or two mixed up in this creature, you'd do nothing but be used as something to empower the creature. Laoni is the only one who can do this."

Natalie tossed the keys to me, and I caught them. "Good luck," she said.

I turned on my heels and ran out the door. I'd only had one real driving lesson, but I had to do my best. I jumped in the bus and sped away from everything. I had no idea what to expect or even if I could find the Neo Breather. I just knew I had to get away from everyone I knew. Natalie had agreed with me.

It was safer for everyone if I made a clean cut.

Cold as ice, even if I didn't have it anymore.

CHAPTER 15

*D*iary,

I freaking miss him! My whole body aches. I'm suffering from withdrawal pains. For a guy. For Redmond. I didn't know it could feel like this. How can anyone survive without the person in their life who they love the most?

I know! This is supposed to be my facts and history to keep a record of my pathetic existence. But I can't even think. I miss him so badly. His hair. His face. The fire in him. How he touched me. I can almost smell him even now in these tunnels under Ybor City in Tampa.

Yes, tunnels. Who knew? Except for the Neo Breather. It knows. It's hiding from me.

Right, I can't just say how much I miss Mond. I want him here, like we were together at the beginning. Alone. We were supposed to be together. How can I feel like this? He's the first guy I've ever loved. First and only. I feel like I've lost my leg or my arm or another body part that I definitely need.

Oops. There I go again.

I followed the trail of the Neo Breather to just outside downtown, where the historic Ybor City exists. I'm getting better at geography. Or maybe it was just because I passed under the large sign proclaiming it as such.

Redmond would be sick of staying put right now. You know, if he were with me.

No! I won't speak about Redmond.

I'm on a stakeout, so to speak. I know the tunnel the Neo Breather has gone into has no exit. It has to come out this way.

The trail wasn't easy to follow. I, get this, had to actually talk to the locals! To humans. They had no idea what I was. But there's been disappearances, and a sweet mother of three told me a story about a monster who sucked her oldest child in.

She led me to these tunnels.

I saw the Neo Breather for one second. Its eyes caught mine— there are a hundred eyes, squashed together. Am I conveying how utterly disgusting this thing is? Let me take another stab at it.

The eyes aren't fully formed ovals. It has eyelids, heavily covered in eyelashes, squashed next to eyeballs, its irises stretched wide. That's not the only grossness. I got a really good look. I thought it would be one big form where a new person would just be sucked in and make the overall form bigger. Nope!

There are multiple arms, all shaped into an overall form of an arm. Millions of fingers together form the overall fingers. Maybe not a million. I am trying to just get the facts! But I can't. Every other word I keep thinking is "Mond."

Mond. Mond. Redmond! He's not my boyfriend anymore. I'm walking the road to death. He's going to live. The Breathers are breathing their last breath these days. No new breeding means no new enemy.

He has a future now, on the island or anywhere he wants.

I don't. Even if he were here, I wouldn't even be able to touch him. I had burned his hand. What would happen if I hugged him, like I desperately need to right now?

Damn it, Laoni! Keep your head together.

Back to the creepy Neo Breather. It has one form, made up of lots of little ones. I came head-to-head with it, lucky for me. We traded blows for about five seconds before it realized I could burn it. Then it fell on its belly and, like a snake, disappeared into the tunnels.

It's smart. It knows that if I follow, it will have the advantages. But the way I see it, it has to come back out sooner or later to eat, to feed the multiple forms. Or to just get another victim.

It needs to kill like I need to eat. Maybe even more.

I'm sitting in this dark tunnel with no real light except from the opening and I'm bored!

That's it. I don't miss Redmond. He isn't my world. He isn't the only reason I draw breath. I'm just bored.

I wish my lies were believable.

Wait, I hear a noise.

The Neo Breather has come to play.

CHAPTER 16

I threw my diary down and flexed my muscles. Right now, this was what I lived for. No thoughts of Redmond. Just me and the beast.

It roared from around the corner, on its belly again, leaving behind a trail of slime. The same stuff it was gestating in…or whatever it was doing.

"Come back for more?" I asked.

"I need food! I need lives!"

Oh, yeah, it could speak. I think I forgot to mention that.

"You need to die. You're not supposed to be. Your life isn't sustainable as it destroys others. Let me put you to sleep."

"Burner enemy! Strip your skin! Suck you in! Become part of me."

"Nah," I stated and made my hand into a claw. I had figured out that that was the best way to make a conduit for my new electricity. I made the lightning into a whip, and it sliced through the air.

The creature was fast! It jumped upward and stuck to the ceiling, its head hanging down to lunge at me.

I jumped backward and whipped through the air.

It rolled, yes, on the ceiling, then slid down the wall like a slimy rubbery eel and came at me.

I fell down and crawled at light speed as it dropped.

"Hungry!" it yelled.

"Me too, but you don't see me complaining about it," I said and aimed for its head. It anticipated that. It moved its body upside down, so its head was on the bottom and its legs on top. My whip snaked through empty air.

"Your death will take a long time! I will eat you slowly, carefully! Your skin will taste so good!"

This was going on my list of nightmares, let me tell you. I aimed for his head again. It rearranged itself. But this time, I was ready. I pulled my electric whip back and then slammed it into its head.

Yes! Direct contact!

It screamed as it sizzled. But it wasn't going to go down just like that. I had paused briefly for my attack. Its many arms in one reached out and grabbed my ankle. Lifting me up into the air, it pulled me to its mouths.

I had done a lot of damage. Its faces were melting, portions of what made it up falling off in withered blackness. But it had me. I shouldn't have let it get that close. I could feel the attempt at melding. My jeans were already slipping into its essence.

"No!" I screamed and lit myself on fire. Electricity, that is. My whole body became a livewire, and it zapped its mouth on energy.

The scream was incredible. A lot of people screaming as one.

"Go ahead!" I yelled as it tried to get loose from my energy. "Eat me!" I started punching the body anywhere I could. My hands blazed, shooting light throughout the small area. Everything I touched shriveled and turned black. The thing was huge.

It took a while.

Finally, I collapsed with piles of black, gross, things around me. And I missed Mond more than ever. My skin felt clammy. I wished I could cry! I closed my eyes and rocked back and forth.

"Wow, I thought you could use some help, but it looks like you didn't need it," a welcomed voice came rushing through my mind.

I opened my eyes to see Redmond there, staring at me.

"How…Why?" I asked.

"Followed you when Natalie wasn't looking, I checked where she sent you."

"Why?" I asked again.

"Because it didn't feel right, you going alone. I am not me without you, okay? Now, is that thing dead? Or do we have to look for it?"

It was gone. Completely disintegrated. "Gone. I've dealt with it."

He had caught me off guard. It's the only excuse I had for what I did. I vaulted up and jumped into his arms, kissing him down his face. "Sorry. Sorry, I'm all goopy."

Redmond drew me in and kissed my neck, my cheek, my chin. "No, you're not."

"Right." Everything had disintegrated when I touched it. There was no slime or goop or Neo Breather left. I had eradicated it. I tried to pull away, but Mond touched me on the waist and I lost all control. I sunk into him, wrapping myself around his body.

"I've missed this!" I murmured.

"Me too. What was up with that anyway?" he asked. "You seemed…" He pulled away. His eyes roved my face. Misery was etched on every feature. "Like you were breaking up with me."

I wished he'd just shut up. Why did he have to look for answers? When he did, they all came back. I had killed the Neo Breather by just touching it. I had burned Mond. And worst of all, I was going to die and hurt him if I didn't kill him first!

I yanked away. "I was. I like Butch." I was pulling out every excuse I could. Butch was so easy. I hadn't even talked to him for more than five seconds and he wasn't my type. My type was tall, blonde, and controlled fire.

"You like him?" Redmond said. "I don't think so. I know you, Laoni. You're not bored of me. You're not! You can't be!"

"Arrogant much?" I demanded. I needed my cold heart. I didn't control ice, but I still had that. "Hey, Mond, we were good together, but as we meet more and more Burners and as life continues on, I see there's more out there. I really wish you hadn't followed me. This relationship is over. Did you really think we'd be together? I mean, come on! We were only sixteen when we met! The chances that we'd be together forever are slim to none."

He was shaking. Fire was burning at his feet, no matter the clothing he wore. "This isn't you. I don't believe it—at all. I get it. You're afraid of hurting me. You burned me, and now you're running scared."

I turned my back on him, rallying all my courage. That wasn't the only reason. I could have been with him forever if so. I would just not touch him. But at least he was angry now. He wasn't devastated. Anger could sustain him until he found someone else.

"I am too young to be tied down," I whispered.

"I don't buy it!" he screamed. "Just tell me you're afraid and we'll get past it. But don't you dare lie to me and say you don't want me! No, you can't."

I heard it in his voice. The pain. The need. He hadn't been wanted. I was doing the same thing everyone in his life had done.

I wasn't ice anymore. I melted.

"Oh, Mond!" I said and turned around. I latched onto him again and pressed everything I had into him. We sank to the floor on our knees. "I'm sorry. I'm so sorry. I want you. I'll never stop."

He only responded by kissing me. We rolled around on the tunnel floor, trying our best to get ever closer.

Mond groaned.

I opened my eyes to see that I was lit up again. Mond was still holding on, but it wasn't because he couldn't move. He didn't care that I was burning his flesh. I wriggled away and shot to the other side of the tunnel, panting. My body screamed at its lost connection.

"We need bandages," I yelped. "You're burned. We shouldn't have touched."

"I'm fine," he argued. "Just a little singed. I'm a fire burner. I heal fast from that. No, really. See my hand."

He waggled his completely healed hand at me. So, it was only temporary. That was at least good.

"I can see why you're scared," he admitted. "That's not a problem. We can work with that. Just don't tell me how much you don't want me and the passion won't build up. We can make this work, Laoni. I mean, maybe Natalie can modify the clothing to work with this new power you've got. Or maybe we could touch in virtual reality. I'd bet there's a way we can be together forever."

I couldn't answer him for a few minutes. I held my elbows together and tried not to explode. "Mond, I'm dying."

Silence filled the small area.

Mond slipped to the ground. I don't know how long we sat there. Maybe hours passed. I wasn't sure. But time was moving. Mond stared at the ground, his face blank of everything but pain.

"Hello?" a new voice asked. "Can we talk?"

That voice. Drake walked into the tunnel.

To say that I was shocked would be an untruth. I'd expected him every single minute I was away from water. I expected him in the bathroom I had hidden away from Redmond in. The thing about Breathers was you could always expect them. My own history gave me that.

"Okay, ready to fight?" I asked. My energy slipped through my skin. Again, I felt uncomfortable. Now that I knew I was dying, I could feel it burning me away.

Drake shook his head. "No. I wanted to bring you back to your mom. I won't fight you."

Redmond appeared unable to function, as though he was still slammed by what I'd said. Wondering if I had meant what I said. Knowing I was telling the truth.

"I don't want to see Mom," I said. Inside I was thrilled. To be wanted. For Mom to send someone to get me? I wept inside. Only inside, though. Outside, I was sharp nails. "In fact, I don't want to see *you*. Go away."

"Wait, I have something to tell you." Drake looked around the tunnel we were in. "Hardly a good hiding spot."

"Tell that to the Neo Breather," I argued. "Or do you not know what that is?"

Drake leaned his extra hot body against the curve of the tunnel and raised his eyebrows. I could see what Mom saw in him. Breathers were as bad as Burners at looking too hot to handle. "I'm not sure what that is. Look, we are not enemies."

I scoffed. I slid down next to Redmond and held his hand, trying to convey how sorry I was that I hadn't told him. And, more importantly, how sorry I was that we had been interrupted so I couldn't tell him the whole story. Drake had exceptionally bad timing, but I wasn't about to tell the truth about my mortality to a Breather who I was pretty sure was a lying jerkbucket.

"Did I come at a bad time?" he asked. "Or do you like hanging out in tunnels with your boyfriend?"

I shot back up. I was ready to rip his face off even if he wasn't my enemy. And yeah, I did. "What do you want? I told you I wouldn't go back. I'll kill you if you want."

Drake chuckled. These Breathers knew how to get under my skin, let me tell you. "No, I don't want that. We left off with things unsaid. After I got your mom and sister to a safe place, I thought I'd look you up. I've never had the scent of a Burner before. It's quite interesting."

"Yes, quite," Redmond said with a sizzling voice. He had recovered. Or at least he had in front of the bad guy. "Thanks for the gun. Got any more?"

He shook his head. "Long story. But it's the only one I could get. Built out of Rider parts but stolen by me."

Okay, now *that* made me jump. "Excuse me?"

"Another long story. Care for some cinnamon candies? I don't go anywhere without them."

This was so ridiculous I just nodded. He tossed me a hard, round candy. I stuck it in my mouth and started moving it around my tongue. The cinnamon was sharp and sweet at the same time. It calmed my nerves.

"Laoni!" Redmond said with his mouth hanging open. "That could have been anything!"

I gave him a *look*, and he got it. What did it matter if it was poison? I wasn't going to recover. Nothing mattered anymore. Luckily, it wasn't poison, just a candy, so Redmond took one too. A strange way to bond with a Breather, all of us making sucking sounds in a tunnel with blackened Neo Breather ash around us.

"Okay, talk. What exactly do you want from me?"

"Me? Nothing." Drake slid down and pushed his feet out in front of him, stretching one toe at a time.

"Every Breather wants a Burner for something," Redmond put in.

"Not me. It's a—"

"Long story, I get it. Okay, then, why are you here?"

He rubbed his jaw and crunched his cinnamon candy in two and brought another to his mouth. "Because I'd do anything for your mom."

I put my finger halfway down my throat. "Gross."

"Love isn't," Drake said simply. "It's pure and wonderful. The point is that your mom wants her daughter back. She never stopped caring about you. She cries in the night. Nightmares affect her sleep." Drake reached backward to scratch his shoulder. I swear if he weren't a Breather, I wouldn't take him for one. This was the first and only time I didn't feel some sinister waves of some kind of need coming off one of them.

It was like…he was human. That wasn't possible! I had seen how these creatures were made—born of evil goop!

But what he was saying carved my insides out. I had hoped Mom would feel guilty. When I was in the facility, I had fantasies when I was trying to go to sleep in that very strange bed. She wanted me. She was looking for me. When I was older, she hated herself for letting me go. And it was all coming true.

"So, she wants me to come be her daughter?"

"Yes, honestly."

I couldn't take this. I held Redmond's hand, hoping my burn wouldn't hurt him. And for this moment, I had my wish granted on two levels. My extermination of the Neo Breather had taken most of the electricity out of me. At least for now. It still was a livewire inside me, fizzing and sparkling, waiting to take me out.

"Tell me, how did you meet her?" I asked.

Drake nodded, as if he expected the question. I don't know, though. Maybe he did. "Only a couple of months after you were taken, I found her at a facility where I was trying to free the Burners. It was hard, because even if I succeeded, most of the Burners could be tracked down."

I wrinkled my forehead. "By their scents?"

He shook his head. "I don't know. The only place any of them could be safe is as fake as a fantasy novel. An island no one has ever heard of."

I chuckled, but only on the inside. Outside, I had narrow eyes and my chin was tight. I wouldn't tell a Breather it was real. I didn't care how nice he sounded. "So, you were trying to save Burners? And then?"

He smiled. I couldn't take this much longer. Drake seemed actually *cuddly* in this moment. The last thing I wanted was to cuddle a Breather. My whole body was tensed. But I wasn't alone. Redmond wasn't taking Drake as a joke either.

"Your mother tried to charge the facility. I mean, she drove her car into the front gate. I knew she was going to be killed. And..." He looked away. He didn't look so cuddly now. He looked angry. "I knew I could save *her* at the very least. Then I got away."

I held up my hand. "You are seriously jumping over details, my man. How'd you escape? And why would you need to? Breathers are a part of that evil."

He gave me a look. "No, they aren't. Even the worst of them have to earn their freedom. They are killed if they decide to leave."

"Oh, goody!" I said. I was ready to rip Drake's head off. "So, you're saying all of the Breathers are poor souls, born into life just to be trapped, and I should feel sorry for them, *right?*"

Drake laughed. "Nope. You should kill them as fast as possible."

I pursed my lips. He was really driving me crazy. "But!"

He held up his hand. "I am not like them. Your mom wasn't lying. I don't even know how out of all my siblings, I had a choice."

My face rippled in disbelief. "A choice of what?"

"Between evil and good. No other Breather has one. They are ready to kill and torture from the moment they are activated. All of them. Every last one except me." Drake's eyes glazed over. The mystery of him wouldn't be solved. But sad to say, I believed him. How many Breathers had I believed? Not one since Farrell.

But I trusted Drake. I was the biggest idiot imaginable.

"To answer your question, I escaped because they believe I'm still working for them. The ones in charge keep an eye on any parents who birth a Burner. They're not sure how the gene comes about, but if a Burner is born, they always have someone watching their family. I just volunteered to watch your mom...closely."

It was a good thing I already trusted him because that line would have caused me to go electric wire on his butt. "And you love her?"

Drake looked at me and honestly said, "Yes. Yes, I do. We created a child together. I didn't even think it was possible. Until you showed up, I was living happily, keeping Scepter from knowing about her. Now, it's too late."

"Who is Scepter? Who's behind the Breathers?"

"It is a group of individuals, but there is one who watches over everything. It is named that because it is the power used by another entity that rules in its place. I've spent my life trying to find out her identity, but all I know is that Scepter has a woman who has complete power. And not just over her organization. She has fingers in the government, military ties, and more. She has slipped into every single organization. Her money grows. Her only purpose is to drain Burners."

"For what?" I demanded. I wondered how much he knew about the Better Suit.

He moved his shoulders to his ears. "I can only guess. But she doesn't want even one Burner left. She wants Breathers in the world. She will let any who does the best work go live a normal life, showers them with money, and doesn't send them on missions. Even for creatures born evil, they still want those perks. All of them seek out Burners for their reward."

I could see why. That only told me that Breathers have logic and reason. They were far from mindless monsters, as Farrell and that creep Digory taught me. I had no cause to feel sorry for any of them.

"I know Scepter sells the energy, using these big battery packs. But I also know that only a few have been sold. Most are sent to the main headquarters for something else."

I couldn't believe how free he was with the information. This was a great asset to us. "For the Better Suit?"

He cocked his head. "The what?"

Redmond laughed. "Don't you know? Whoever is behind all this, they're making a wonderful thing to wear to formal functions."

Drake smiled. "That sounds ridiculous."

It did to me as well. No one would take energy stolen from Burners just to put it into some fancy apparel. There was something more here. And something Drake said bothered me.

"You said they kept an eye on anyone who had a Burner child. For how long? I mean, do they give up after they take the Burner away? Or is it a lifetime type of thing?"

Drake stared at me. "It's a lifetime type of thing. Or at

least as long as the parents can have children. They don't take chances."

Redmond and I shared a look and jumped up. "The Barclays!"

"Wait, where are you going?" Drake demanded. "I promised I'd bring you back. Your mom needs you."

"Too bad. Got a job to do."

"I won't go back empty-handed," Drake said. Wow, now I could tell he was a Breather. He had the same angry undertone, the same refusal to give up.

"Fight us then." I ran toward the exit. I had parked the bus far down the street away from the tunnels. Mond and I ran side by side. "Are we thinking this is doomed?" I asked, feeling like my skin was way too tight.

"I'm thinking, yes. If they have a watcher on the family, they know we're there." Redmond slid into the driver's seat. I didn't mind. I had barely gotten it here. I was way better at driving than before, but I didn't care for all the stuff I had to remember.

And I was scared. My whole team was there. More were coming. The second team sent by Nora. What if…?

To my surprise, Drake jumped in the back. "Hey, if you won't come with me, I'll just dog your tracks until you do. I told you, I won't go back empty-handed. It also seems you have an issue. You might need me."

I scoffed but didn't do anything as Redmond floored it. We just didn't have time. Dread roared up in my stomach.

The day welcomed our bus down the road. We drove. We would be too late. I just knew it.

CHAPTER 17

*D*iary,

I can't...Sorry. Froze up for a minute there. For the longest time, I've turned to you when life just was too much. When too many big thoughts crowded my brain. And I have to now.

But where do I start? I've faced death. Faced pain. Even faced a machine that turned me into a new being that's going to die. But this new stuff is hard for even me.

Okay, I'll start with where I am. I'm about three miles from a Breather breeding ground. Why, you ask? Because that's where my friends have been taken.

Yes, taken. The Barclays were being watched. The problem is four teen Burners and an old one weren't much of a prize. They had hoped we'd lead them to where we took all the ones we rescued.

When Nora's team showed up, they attacked. How do I know this? Because...

This hasn't happened before. I can't seem to write. I just keep stopping. Maybe because once I write it down, it will be recorded. It will be real.

Okay. Here I go again. The Barclays are all gone. The Burners are gone. Taken away by Breathers, I guess...

S-shaking to-oo hard to write. Redmond is holding my arm, trying to sleep. But as usual, I can't. I'm shoved as tightly against the back of the bus as possible, away from our ally, the supposed "good Breather." After what happened, I should kill him. As slowly and as painfully as I can muster. I can't trust Breathers. But this time, I have no choice. Drake knows where to go—a rescue mission.

Oh, right, back to what happened. We returned to a wasteland. The house was destroyed. The only person left told me what happened.

Babs gasped out her last words, telling us the story.

A Flyer came—lots of Flyers. The two groups of Burners fought them, and even the Barclays fought. When it was over, their house was rubble, and Babs was left to die.

We did our best to save her—fat lot of good that did. She died in my arms, begging me to save her children. It turns out...Diary! I'm sick of writing things like this! Everywhere I go, people die. I've led Breathers to my location and had innocents pay the price before, but this was the first time they had faces. Names. A family that had brought us all in.

I'm sick of it! I don't want...

Right. Too emotional. What happened. During the attack, Flyers swooped down and grabbed Burners one by one and flew off. They didn't care when their faces were ripped off by flying shrapnel. Had only one goal in mind. Capture and retreat.

I could barely hear Babs' whispers telling us what had happened. Redmond had fallen to his knees behind me, unable to take all this in. I'm the only one who'd experienced this kind of pain. He had seen people die thanks to his explosion, but again, he hadn't really caused it. It had been his drunken father.

I had two roles yesterday, Diary. One, comfort a dying woman; and two, comfort my boyfriend, who was beyond comfort. I wasn't good at either.

Anyway, focus. Focus. I need to focus. I can't give in to this. Not me. I am strong!

Babs begged me to save her children. Yes, all of them were taken away. Babs and Ralph were the ones killed. Ralph, by the first attack, shot down by a Flyer.

I owe Babs. She stayed alive long enough to give us the information we needed. Drake knows where they'd be taken. The only place close enough to house the prisoners. The facilities with the machines are too far away, so he thinks they've been taken north, toward the next breeding ground, somewhere in North Carolina. I don't care exactly where. Geography, not my strong suit. I'm not sure what exactly is.

I'm losing who I am, to be honest, and if I can't be here, then where can I be? I didn't know how much my ice had made me who I am. Since I was little, I could always rely on it. Even when it was taken away from me, forced out by the clothing that blocked it, I still felt it there. Now? All I feel is energy. I can't even let it out to make art. It's all just roiling inside me.

A noise!

Oh, just a bird flying past. I'm on edge. I am so sick of people dying. That's it! No more humans. None. I can't risk them anymore. Had we just found a better hideout, they'd be alive. Babs and Ralph.

I know what I have to do. Protect them. Babs' last words were, "I couldn't save Erin. Please tell me you will." I promised her. Erin has to be rescued. So do Butch and Carolyn.

But how do we save them? If we go in blazing, they most likely will be killed. Even if we do save them, where can we send them? The island is for Burners, not humans. Would they be welcomed in?

Wow...Everything sounds so simple when I write it down. Save the rest of the Barclays. Protect Erin.

It's not simple. It's the most complicated thing I've ever done.

Why can't I sleep?

I'm going to wrap myself around Mond for a while. I hope I will fall asleep and not burn him. I need him tonight.

Diary, no more death. I swear it. None will die if I'm there.

Those Breathers don't know who they're messing with. The one behind this doesn't know me, but I plan to show her who I am.

CHAPTER 18

I woke up to Redmond staring at me. I quickly checked him over. Good. No burns. Maybe I had been too wiped out. I can't believe I actually slept, as fitful as it was. Babs closed her eyes for the last time a hundred times in my mind.

"I'm okay," he said. He opened up the back of the bus and gestured for us to walk. Drake was still asleep. We were at a quiet rest stop with no other cars. Redmond still had driven past the parking lot and got out of view. So, we were surrounded by trees.

We crunched along the forest floor for a while. My skin felt hot and clammy. I wasn't one for humidity!

"How do you know?" Redmond asked.

I knew what he was asking.

"I'm an Alternate Burner. I am burning too fast for my body to handle. The more I fight, the more I use. I'm like a battery. Sooner or later, I'll wear out."

Redmond nodded. "Is there a way to stop it? Use your powers less?"

The pain in his voice touched me. I drew him in and held

my cheek against his heart. It beat steadily, strong. "Mond, we're going into battle. We're trying to save a whole lot of our friends. This isn't the time."

Mond grasped the back of my head. He held me so tightly I couldn't move. My heart ached at his ferocity. "I don't care. If you can use your powers less and live, let me and Drake free them. You go back to the island. Put your feet up. Have everyone wait on you hand and foot. You can't die. No. Not an option."

I touched my hands as they encircled his waist and swayed in time to the beating of his heart. We couldn't stay like this for long. I could feel my energy more than ever. Mond was holding onto a livewire that was currently insulated. But if I held him for much longer, I'd hurt him.

"Mond, do you really think I could do that? You need me. You should have seen that Neo Breather go down."

Mond pulled away and glared at me. "It's your life! Can you stop the, uh, countdown if you don't fight? If you don't use your powers?"

I considered. Natalie hadn't said anything about that. "At best, I could delay it. But I couldn't do that."

"Yes, you could." I was wounding him. His voice was a bleeding hole. "If I asked you to. If you wanted to stay alive for me."

I let him go. I knew when I'd burn him. I was too close. He didn't release me, though. "For your own safety," I whispered. "Let me go."

He let his arms fall, and I backed away.

"Is that because you're going to hurt me? Or because you're going to die? I mean, that is the reason you didn't tell me before, isn't it? Instead, you ran away. You let me believe..."

"Yeah, and think!" I said. The sun filtered through the trees, dappling his face. Making his blond hair look dark in patches and light in others. "If you hated me, you wouldn't have to watch me die. And you will. Because I can't let you go into battle without me. I can't imagine betraying any of my friends. Not again. You know how I abandoned them before. You were the one who wanted me to go back to save them! I have to do that again."

Mond deflated. He knew my answer. "But you're wrong. I wouldn't have been happy to find out later you had lied to me to save me. I would have hated finding out like that. At least this way, if I can hold your hand as you go out, then I'll be complete. You shouldn't have made that decision for me. If you have to die…"

His face crumpled. He slammed his fists into a tree and singed two hand-shaped holes. "Then I want to be there. I need to say goodbye."

I walked over to the tree and slammed my smaller fists under his. I overlapped them and I sent my own energy into the tree. "We'll always be together now," I said, gesturing to the tree. "My fists and yours in union on this tree."

He tried to smile, but turned away. He didn't want me to see his tears.

"Besides, you are being very presumptuous to think either of us will survive a direct attack on a Breathers' place without any backup except a Breather I'm pretty sure is going to betray us. For all you know, you'll die first."

"If only!" Mond said. He had a wet smile when he looked back. "But I think you're wrong about Drake. He seems…nice."

"Bite your tongue!" I snapped.

He was silent. Then he gave me a smile that would have melted me, had I still been ice. "How long?"

"I don't know." I felt throughout my body. "A year, maybe? Two, tops. But how much I use is a factor."

"Then be careful. Because we're going to save them all.

We're going to make it. And I want to make your last two years the best ever. When you go toward that dark night, I…"

He didn't finish. He didn't have to. I knew what he was saying. "No. Mond, you will find a friend. One that doesn't mind the ghost of me on your mind. You will have children. You will continue the line of the Burners. I want to know that despite the evil around us, the need for our destruction, the forces against us, that we will survive. We will be a part of this world. We will show the humans what we are, and we will be accepted. One day. I want that as my legacy. You can't deny me that by dying with me. Please…"

I was begging at the end. It ripped apart my soul to imagine Mond married to someone else. Having her children. But I wanted it more than I ever thought possible. My family had been ripped apart. Erin's had been. And I knew that across the country, maybe the world, there were families being ruined by this. I wanted to imagine that someday, it wouldn't be like that.

Then I could die happily.

"I promise," he said. "I'll do it for you. But my happiness dies with you. You understand that?"

I did. We had touched each other too deeply. I knew I'd feel the same.

We didn't touch as we walked back to the bus. Drake was just waking up. It was time to move on again.

～

Drake balanced a burger on his knee as he checked over the map. We couldn't stop for food, so we resorted to fast food. I almost missed the frozen block I used to eat. This stuff was nasty.

"Okay, so this one is underground," he said. "It was too

113

close to traffic, so they needed to camouflage it."

"Okay, then, what's our plan?" Redmond asked. "Dig it up?" He laughed at his own joke. He had completely shut off worries about the future. Now that he knew I had an expiration date, he had put it out of his mind and focused on our mission. He was right. I should never have hidden my death from him. He had the right to know. And he could put it away for the time being.

"First things first. You need information. I'm guessing you don't know what's guarding it or why they kept some of the Barclays alive?"

I shook my head. I almost couldn't believe he was going to just tell us. As I stared at him, he was becoming an ally. How could I trust him? The last time I trusted any Breather, I almost died because of it. And one of my friends *had*.

Drake smiled. He had my undivided attention, and he sure was showing off. "Okay, you have to understand that there are three types of Breathers."

I held my hand up, took a bite of my nasty burger, swallowed painfully, and then spoke. "Yeah. Rider, Flyer, and Runner. The last has two types, Bloodhound and just the normal pain in the butt."

Drake nodded. "Yes, but although they share the same name, they are very different. The Breathers are bred. The Flyers are made. The Riders come from a different place."

So simple. But, all of a sudden, my life got a whole lot more complicated. I should have known. At the breeding grounds, I had only seen the two types, Runner and Bloodhound. I could almost pick them out of a crowd now. No Flyers. No Riders. That meant...a whole lot. But mostly, it meant that the breeding grounds were going to get a whole lot tougher.

I closed my eyes. "So, let's begin with the Flyers. How are they...?"

Drake looked grim. Almost angry. He didn't like this any more than I did. "The Flyers are forced into existence. The Scepter takes human beings and augments them with certain types of machinery. The same origin as the gun I gave you."

I nodded. Nothing could shock me now. I had kind of that feeling. The Flyers were so…different.

"When Flyers are sent, they are programmed, which bypasses any human thought. Once they complete their mission, they go back to the brain they had, remembering everything."

I held my stomach. This was making me sick. If I killed a Flyer—if I could—I'd be killing an innocent human. And I knew it wouldn't stop me. Nothing would.

"Okay, so that makes sense, I guess. But…" I stopped as Drake looked at me with a withering expression. "What?"

"You want to just move on. You're quite impatient."

I gave a little hiss. He, of course, ignored me. "The Flyers' origins are important." He finished his burger. Shoving the wrapper into the bag, he handed it to me so I could put mine in as well. Redmond just burned the whole thing when I handed it to him. No waste.

"I don't care that they used to be human."

Drake sighed. "It's not just that. Information is power. You can choose what to do with it. Having a choice gives freedom. The Flyers are used against their will, forced into doing battle. Not like the other Breathers who choose but always choose evil. Flyers have no choice. Most of them shut down because what's the use in fighting something that can order you to kill even your best friend? But when they are aware, un-programmed, they can aid us. That's when we use them."

I gave a little smile. Drake was a man after my own heart. "You're saying that if we can communicate with them, they might turn on their owners?"

Drake clapped his hands together, "Exactly! But there's something you keep missing."

"Then enlighten me, oh smart one," I said.

"That's why the remaining Barclays were captured. The genes that make Burners also give a nice compatibility with the computer shoved into their brain. They killed the parents because they wouldn't adapt. But they kept the children."

Okay, that burger was really hard on my stomach. I had to keep it together. I didn't want to throw up. But I saw it so clearly. The Flyers that came after me, human, living nicely, kidnapped and assaulted. Forced to work for the very entity that ruined them. Now Butch and Carolyn would be...

"How much time does it take?" I demanded.

"Days. It's a highly precise operation, connecting the mechanical parts to the human brain. But if they made them a top priority, and since they're so young, it could take mere hours. They could already be hooked up. That means you'll have to fight them."

I jumped up and shoved the bus's doors open. We had found a place on the side of the road, blocked from the highway by a huge sign. We were almost to our destination. Now I had to worry about having to fight and kill the very people I needed to save.

"Hold on," Drake said, right next to me. He took his own life in his hands and put a comforting palm on my shoulder. I stiffened but didn't move. "There is still so much more."

"What?" I flipped his hand off my shoulder. "I can't take much more. Are you going to tell me that Erin and Cindy, Natalie, and all the others will be Flyers, too?"

"No. Burners can't be modified. All that can be done with them is draining." Drake crossed his arms and gave me a gentle push. I sat down on the edge of the end of the bus.

"Some advice? You're letting emotion get in the way. Not safe. It can kill you."

I fought the urge to say, *Well, duh.*

"Go in your mind. Take it and turn it into stone. It can be softened when you're done, but imagine all your pains, fears, and anything else like they don't exist. Turn your emotion into conviction."

I tried to take his advice. There was so much! It was burying me. But Erin would be fine. Yes, that was better. All of them would be fine. I'd save them. Erin lost her parents, but she still had her brother and sister. There was still time. I wouldn't have been given that time if there was no hope.

The powers-that-be wouldn't be that cruel.

I sucked everything inside. My brain was stone. I'd fight. Hadn't I been almost born to do that? I couldn't be ruined now. Not when there were still battles to be fought!

"Okay, what else?"

Redmond laughed. "Hey, can you lend me some of your moxie? Because I can't just shut off like you can."

"You don't have to, boy," Drake said. "When there's someone else to lead you, you have the luxury of just following orders."

Redmond glared at him. "Don't call me boy." Then he glanced at me. "I'll follow you anywhere."

More pressure. More layers of my rock. "Okay, good."

Redmond didn't know it, but he was my real rock. If he had faith in me, I had faith in me. "Tell me the rest."

"Riders are behind any of the technology you've seen. The machine that ripped your essence out of you. The motorcycles that transform. The gun. The Flyers."

"Uh-huh, and where do *they* come from," Redmond asked, "if they can make such crazy things? I saw this motorcycle completely surround my car."

I raised an eyebrow. "*Your* car?"

Redmond laughed. "I rightfully stole it. But that stuff is bad with a capital B. How? And how many times can they do that?"

Funny. Redmond admired me, but right now, I admired him. He was keeping a sense of humor. He was transforming. He had been a real pessimist when I met him, wondering when the next bad thing would happen. Since he had been with me, the bad things had increased and gotten worse, and yet he forced himself to keep the optimism. He wouldn't get down. I was lucky.

"As for how?" Drake shrugged and scratched his jaw. It was getting scruffy. I was always amazed at how human Breathers were, and even more so after seeing that disgusting, weird-ass creation of them. "It's not possible. Not on Earth," he said meaningfully.

I threw my head into my hands. "They're aliens?"

Drake pushed out a tight smile. "Don't call *them* that. They take it as an offense. When humans usually think of aliens, little green men pop up or grotesque monsters that will rip your throat out."

"I've met Riders who would have been glad to do just that," I argued.

"The point is, do not take them lightly. They're moody, emotional, prone to tantrums. They love hunting down Burners. Scepter came together when they found someone who hated Burners as much as they did."

"How did she find them?" I kept asking questions. I shouldn't have. It was wasting time. We needed a strategy. And the more answers only made my rock inside falter.

"I don't know." Drake stood up and looked at the trash-filled field around us. "I'm not privy to everything. I have a Flyer contact inside. She gives me what I need to know. But the secrets about the Riders and the identity of the leader of Scepter is all a closely guarded secret."

Drake had a Flyer contact inside. Great. A whole bunch of friends that I'd have to treat like enemies if I encountered them.

"Where is your contact?" I demanded. "At our destination? Or…"

Drake sighed. "Yes. She is. She is at the Flyer Adaption Services, the underground facility that forces humans to become Flyers. The very place we'll attack."

"Yes, *we*." I stared at him. "You only came to get me back to my mom. Why would you switch so fast?"

"You have no idea who I am!" he said. He slammed the back of the van. "You think I'm like *them*? I'm not. They disgust me. I have morals. I have a conscience. It would have been better for me if I had been born like the rest, only living for thrills. Loving the scent of Burners in my nose. But I don't. I chose life. I chose family. And…" He jabbed with his first finger at the empty space to the left of us, but I knew he was really pointing to a ruined house that lay in rubble and the body we had found.

"That was a family. It could be mine. It will be. I've been working against that place all my life. Secretly sneaking in. Working double-time just so your mother wouldn't have to be risked. Looking for *you*!"

"But you never found me."

Drake shook his head. "No. I'm a failure. I just hope I can someday be a success."

My heart trilled in sympathy. How many times did I feel that way about myself? Fighting the same enemy. Failing at every turn. But I had a few successes now. Drake had none. If I had stayed put, would he have found me? Would he have brought me home to my mom?

"Drake, how do we attack?" I asked.

Something in my voice made him stare at me. I was just offering my friendship, but he took it as so much more.

Like…he had adopted me so long ago when he started the search. A father…

"Inside and out. We need all the firepower we can muster. I'll contact the Flyer inside. I hope she's not programmed today. She'll open the door. We go in. Kill everything you see and head toward…"

Drake shook his head. He scuffed some grass off the dirt and sketched out a crude diagram of the building we were going to. Tunnels that went out right and left and all dead-ended in small blind rooms. The biggest one was where the Flyers were modified. The others were rooms where they were hooked up, charging for when they'd be used again.

"This room is where the Barclays will be. Your friends will be in the prison, which is here, down one staircase that goes even lower into the bowels of the Earth."

"Eww," Redmond joked.

I smiled. "Okay, so we split up. Redmond, you go after our friends. You get them, and they can help you. Go fast. Don't stop. Burn everything."

"Ooh, what I live for," he said with wiggling eyebrows.

I tried not to laugh. This situation was too serious. But the funny thing was when you shut off fears, worries, and pain, you can only laugh at anything ridiculous.

"I'll take on the Flyers in the making room."

Drake gestured wildly as if to say what about me?

"Come on, Drake. You know what you have to do. Stay outside and be our getaway. As far as I know, the only thing Breathers can do is die. So, whatever."

"How little you know," he retorted. He pushed a button on his belt and suddenly it snaked off and recoiled into a weapon. "We can fight—that's what we're meant to do. Fight and track. Let's do this."

So, we were on.

The building was, in all honesty, a door—just a door in the side of a small mound of dirt. Like I said before, the entirety of the place was underground. Once we were standing on the doorstep, Drake got in touch with his contact. She opened the door for us. One of the only things to go right from then on.

We rushed inside, reached an intersection, nodded at each other like old army buddies, and separated. Thanks to Drake's crude design, I got where I wanted to go. The tunnels hung low, reminding me well that I was under lots and lots of dirt. As I went deeper, I grew more claustrophobic. Luckily for me, I was attacked left and right by Breathers. This was the Flyer facility, but none were on duty. I guess because the Flyers were only brought out for special occasions.

I might have missed my ice, but when a Breather shot toward me, weapons blaring, all I had to do was toss my lightning at them and they were out of my hair.

I didn't stop running, fueled by fear and need. Worry. Could Redmond get my people out? Would I find Butch and

Carolyn okay? I was fighting, but those questions still shot through my mind.

I ducked down as a beam of energy shot over my head. Falling to the miniature tiled floor, I skidded a few paces as I wildly reached out. Every time I shot lightning, my body turned on. I was becoming light.

"Wow, you've changed," a voice said. *Great, Paul again.* I didn't even know him, but he sure wanted to get to know me.

"Hello, Paul. You do know you're dead, right?" I said, getting to my feet.

"Not today," he said casually and tossed a little silver ball into the air. I watched it arc and fall, shining in the overhead lamps. I caught it in my left hand and encased it. Then it exploded.

I took all the energy into my hand.

Impossible.

Paul looked like he felt the same way. As usual, he was good-looking. A curtain of shaggy brown hair, a chiseled jaw with a nicely indented cleft, and piercing eyes that could make any woman blush.

"How?" he asked.

"Never met an Alternate Burner before, have you? Now, either get out of my way or die. Your choice."

He skirted the tunnel wall, backing up until he reached a place he could run. "I'll see you again," he said. "You're going after another breeding ground. That's where we'll meet up again."

Okay, Paul was a strange one. All the other Breathers were, well, not cowards. This guy was a runner, which also meant he was a survivor. Good for him. Bad for me.

"You try to kill me again and I'll end your life, got me?" I asked.

Paul grinned. "We'll see. I personally look forward to

shoving you back into a machine. Maybe this time we can get it right." He ducked and ran before my lightning could hit him.

Why did certain bad guys have to keep coming back? Oh well. He wasn't a problem now.

I continued my run. The ground dipped lower and lower. All through the tunnel, there were fake windows showing fake vistas—beaches, forests, cityscapes, sky. I guess even Breathers got bored of not seeing the outside.

But to me, it was unsettling to go from a city view to a forest. Like it was trying to trick me that I was not where I was. I felt the massive amounts of earth around me.

The door to the place I trying to get to was heavily guarded. I didn't care. I was invincible. I was so lit up, I caught my reflection on one of the fake windows. I was like humanoid electricity. I could barely even see my features.

The door came up. I shot three Breathers to the side and sent two tendrils of electricity to pry open a heavy security door.

I was so glad I couldn't pause to take a breath. The power inside me took even my breath away.

The interior held rows of tables. A mad scientist's lab of horrors. There were bodies on the tables, some of which had white sheets over their heads. Others were alive, but unconscious. Long tubes with pointed needles on the ends stuck inside the brains of the latter. Shaved skulls showed the access points. Inside the clear tubes, I saw only silver. But I had no idea what it was.

Maybe little streams of nanotechnology? Maybe silver poison. Who knew?

I took out the lab technicians before I realized they were human. Not Breathers. It didn't matter. Not now.

The quiet settled on me.

I was surrounded by bodies, alive and dead. Some caused by me, some caused by the ones I killed.

I hoped Butch and Carolyn weren't under those sheets!

To my relief, as I looked across the large room of white and silver, I saw at the far end two familiar faces. I ran over to them. Their eyes were plastered shut. Butch's head had been completely shaved while Carolyn's was halfway done.

As I looked at Carolyn's little body prostrate on that table, I couldn't help but think of *my* little sister. The way she was afraid of me the last time I had seen her. Gem. If she were on this table…If she were ever caught…

I smoothed my brow and wondered if I were to pull the needles out, what damage could I cause?

"You'll have to disconnect them from the machines before you do anything else."

I jumped almost to the moon.

I spun around. "Who the hell are you?" I demanded. A tallish girl stood against the wall. She couldn't be older than seventeen.

I wasn't afraid, even if I did see these creatures nightly in my nightmares. She was a Flyer. She wore a completely gray suit. From her neck to her scalp was a panel like you'd see on a security door. Lots of buttons and a touchpad—for her to be programmed.

Her hair was still shaved from where she had been augmented. But the hair on the other side of her head was a black bob that barely touched her shoulders.

"My name is unimportant now. I am a slave to my masters. I'm told when to move and put away when I'm done."

For some reason, that hurt. For her to not even register her own name! "What did it *used* to be?"

She cocked her head. "You are a Burner. Drake told me you were coming with his message. You are here to save lives. Yet, you ask me my name. I have lost it. Long ago. If you'd like, when they programmed me, they called me 0142."

I wrinkled my nose. I didn't know why her name was so important to me. There was danger all around. Just because I was doing well didn't mean I was out of the woods. But everyone should know their own name. To identify themselves as different from everyone else.

I shook my head. I had to focus. Butch and Carolyn depended on me. "So, you're the contact inside. Can you help me?"

She shook her head. Was it my imagination or did I hear a whirring when she moved? More machine than human? Or more human than machine?

"I can give you information. I can't help anyone escape. It is against my programming. These new arrivals have already been transformed. The Nanoments are ripping through their brains. Unplug them now, and it will halt the process. Maybe natural healing can take place and shove the foreign elements out. But you'll have to work quickly. See that computer console?"

I looked to where she was pointing. It was a large, blank screen with a built-in keyboard and a touch mouse. But if I touched it...I was still lit up like a Christmas tree. I had no idea how to shut it down.

"Umm, can you...?" I asked.

Again, 0142 shook her head. "I am not programmed to handle this equipment. More so, I am forbidden to touch it."

I looked at my hands. Small suns. Energy that could and would zap the very thing I needed to unhook my friends.

"Intruder. Must be eliminated."

Aw, crap. Like things couldn't get so much worse!

I turned around to see that my information giver, my new friend, 0142, was completely changed. She shot her tentacles at me. I had no idea where she had hidden them before.

But as I expected, the tentacles hit the living barrier of electricity I had and wiggled and quivered. It traveled up into her body and sent her into convulsions. This was just great!

I ran over to her and watched as the electricity in her squiggled away to nothing. Her eyes were wide open, flashing between red and humanoid.

She blinked!

"Hey, 0142, you okay? You still want to kill me?"

"I…was…programmed to stop intruders. I fought…it." Her lips formed a smile. I was a little shocked to see normal teeth. I guess she hadn't gotten the Flyer teeth somehow.

Red flashed and then went away again.

"What did I do to you?" I asked, trying to ignore the body of the scientist I had killed on the way in. He was only a few paces away from the body of the Flyer.

"Short circuit. I won't kill you." A flicker of emotion touched her eyes. "You…destroyed…the link."

I held my sparking hands together. "You can be programmed remotely. Someone is controlling you?"

0142 twitched. I took that as a no.

"You are my savior."

Suddenly, she leaped up and started leaning on a table. She was so heavy, she shoved it over, complete with sheet-covered body. Too many freaking bodies.

"Save your friends," she said and drunkenly scooted over to the computer terminal. With a few jabs, she brought the system online and tapped a command.

A whining noise hit as the needles withdrew. I walked over to Butch, and 0142 followed.

"Wake them up," I said. I heard a noise outside. If 0142

could be programmed from afar, then the alarm had been sounded. They knew we were here. Maybe it was Paul. Maybe it was Scepter. But there were a whole lot of Flyers out there.

"Very well," she said and slapped Butch!

"Ow!" he groaned and sat up.

My mouth gaped. "Not the best way to do that. Butch, could you wake up Carolyn. Gently," I added with a look at 0142.

He was so out of it, all he could do was follow my orders. He shook Carolyn, who woke disoriented. "What's going on?"

I wondered how much they knew. "Your parents…"

Butch gritted his teeth. "We were attacked. They're dead, aren't they?"

"No!" Carolyn yelled.

"Stop!" I ordered. "There's no time for grief. Outside, there are lots of Flyers. We need to get out of here. Stay behind me. Stay alert, and don't mourn. There'll be time for that later."

"Is Erin alive?" Carolyn begged.

I didn't have the heart to tell her that I didn't know. That worried me too.

Suddenly, a loud, angry, beeping noise echoed. The room around me shook like an earthquake was coming. I ducked down as the roof above us started sliding.

Sky met my gaze. The whole place had been opened up. Of course! The Flyers were here. They needed a place to take off from. And take off they did. All around, one by one, bodies flew into the sky.

"Must eliminate intruders."

I looked across the now sheered top of the lab and saw Redmond and…

All of them! My friends. Bobby. Natalie. Erin! Cindy.

They were alive! Oh, but not for long. The Flyers' eyes turned red.

"Kill switch is on," the metallic voices said in unison.

"The order for complete elimination has been given," 0142 said emotionless at my ear.

"Yeah, I got that," I said.

I heard the sound of weapons being cocked. They were trained on Erin. On the person I'd promised to save. No!

I leaped into the air…

And I flew. Yes, I flew. I had no idea how I could. I didn't even know I could. But I hovered like the Flyers.

"Come on!" I screamed. "I'm the intruder. Eliminate me!" Then I shot through the sky, slamming into one Flyer after another.

I was on fire. Or on electricity, whatever. I felt the computers in the Flyers going out. *Phzz. Swish. Crackle.*

They fell. All of them. I lit up the entire area, shooting through each and every one. In my own way, I was destroying another breeding ground. I ripped the Flyers out of the sky.

Then I crackled out.

I fell.

To my surprise, 0142 shot up next to me and caught me, letting me down gently. "You saved me. I will save you."

I gave a weak grin. I was out of energy. But not like before. I was still standing. I had saved them all.

A mighty cheer broke out, the group's relief was evident as their fear dissipated. They were yelling *my* name. Wow, interesting, considering I was a murderer of every kind of person.

"Can we get out of here?" I asked.

They were surprised by my tone. But this battle wasn't over. Whoever had been controlling the Flyers was still out there. And there was still one more breeding ground—the Riders.

I wasn't done. I'd never be done.

We left 0142 with the Flyers, who were alive but out of it. Hopefully, she could help them with their new lives. We had more important stuff to do. Redmond held my hand as we tried to shove everyone into the small bus. It'd be tight, but it'd get us out of there.

"Nice hair," he said. I could hear all the unspoken thoughts. But I looked at him with confusion.

He pointed at the mirror on the side of the bus. I gasped. A whole section of my hair had been transformed from white to black. A startling contrast. "How?"

"You're burning out," Natalie mentioned from behind us.

I didn't want to hear it. They had reserved the passenger seat for the hero, for me, and I slid into it, trying to ignore the cramped people behind me. "We need a hideout."

Natalie took the driver's seat and we were off.

But she was right. I felt older. More used up. I *was* dying. And every time I used my energy, I used up more of my inner supply.

But as Mond kept his hand on my shoulder, massaging my neck tension, it was almost worth it.

CHAPTER 20

*D*iary,

Phew! I finally have a chance to take a breath. With two breeding grounds destroyed, no new Breathers will be made to come after us, giving us much more of a chance at surviving this. The others, at least. I'm...Well, I'm not going to whine.

Of course, the Flyers aren't all wiped out. But I guess I short-circuited them enough to stop any future commands. 0142 is staying behind and getting them all to safety in whatever way she can. Not my problem. As long as they aren't coming after us.

Where am I? My mom's new place. I know, I know. You're asking what I'm doing here. Me, too. But Drake, sheesh, he is not to be annoyed. He wanted me back, and he seriously dogged my every step until I agreed. And since he knows my scent, he can be even more of a nuisance than any other Breather.

So, I finally screamed at him when he walked in on me and Redmond making the best of my drained state. I agreed to come home, and he just smiled and said he'd get us a vehicle.

The bus is staying with Natalie. That thing is amazing. It's still running. Oh, yeah, everyone was fine. I'm amazed at our good luck. Natalie and the rest of the Burners were locked up. Paul was talking about transferring them to another facility when I showed up.

Needless to say, that plan changed.

Victory! Success! Erin reunited with her siblings. It hurts to watch them grieve their parents. I'm amazed they have a chance. Drake is helpful, at least. He gave us a new hideout. He brought us to an artificial dam that has a perfect buried space underneath it. According to him, it was part of old records that none of the Breathers use anymore. The place has rooms and stuff. Like a gift from the gods...The water masks all of us. The rooms give us a home. Natalie has been in and out a lot, getting supplies to stay here. We need a good place to hide while we're planning the next move.

Problem. We have no idea where the Riders' breeding ground is. More info seeking. More time taken. Plenty of time for me to take a vacation at my mom's place.

You know, Diary, I'm on edge as I write this. Erin can really get inside my head, and she is more pessimistic than ever before. I'd be the same if I'd watched my parents get killed when I'd just found them again. But she watched me run to my diary right after we got settled in and she said, "Aren't you afraid that the diary will fall into the wrong hands and they'll know all about us and our weaknesses, not to mention your secret thoughts and feelings?"

Well, no, Diary, I hadn't been before! Now, I'm terrified. My own outlet to let it all show, and I have to be nervous. No. I won't be Erin. I'll keep it safe. It's mine. And people will have to go through me to get it.

I won't stop writing in this. I won't code my words. I can't. I need someone to talk to.

I guess I should let Mond know what I'm thinking. He is closer to me than anyone, but I like being strong in his eyes, and I am so weak here.

Let's see...

Mom's house is nice. It's surrounded by trees. I believe we're in New Hampshire, but my geography-lacking brain and I don't care.

We just arrived this morning. Mom said it was okay if we all got settled. She even gave me and Mond rooms next to each other. But she expects us to sleep in our own rooms. Yeah, sure. Mom, I'm seventeen now, not six. I won't listen.

I feel bad. Just that. Bad. I'm dying. Mom doesn't know it yet. She's already talking about going on a vacation together. She wants me to think about moving in when everything is done. My sister looks at me with big eyes, not too sure about me, I guess.

Yeah. I was the one who arrived and made her whole world explode.

It's disgusting to see the three of them. Because I'm bitter. But, yeah, Diary, it's actually wonderful to see them all together. Drake loves my mom so much, and he loves Gem too. A Breather actually caring. It turns my stomach.

I'm afraid for tomorrow. Mom wants to talk to me. Really talk. I don't even know what about. We're strangers. I saw her last when she was terrified of me, as Farrell dragged me off and I begged her to save me.

Then so many years passed. Eleven, and here we are.

You know what the scariest thing is, Diary? I want to forgive her. I want to let it all go. I'm dying. I want it all peaceful when I go. But how can I forgive the woman who ruined my life?

Oh, Mond's sneaking in. Gotta go.

CHAPTER 21

I stared at Mom, taking in her face. It was so lovely. I looked a lot like her. Same high forehead and faint but defined cheekbones. A living mark that I wasn't alone in this world. I had come from her.

Mom's dining room was a thing of beauty. There was a long thin dining table, complete with a lacey table runner. The windows all around showed the green mass that encroached upon this place. The wood of the table was shiny and smelled earthy and nice. The floor, a beautiful red marble, held throw rugs of ash and gold. Through two archways was the rest of the house, but it was the dining room that was the focal point of the whole house.

I was placed across from Mom while my sister and Drake were on Mom's side. Mond was next to me as usual. I couldn't believe she had set up this new place so quickly after the destruction of the old.

"This is my second home," she said nervously.

"Ah, from the million," I answered cruelly.

Mom blushed.

Drake stepped in. "No, she spent that looking for you. I

was the one who siphoned off money for years from the big ones."

I shook my head. "And used it for yourself?"

"Oh, the runaway thief is judging me," Drake said. "The point is, Scepter doesn't have it and my family is safe. Wouldn't you do the same?"

I would. And my stomach softened a bit at the idea that Mom didn't use that money for luxury.

"Okay, so…" I shoved a forkful of scrambled eggs into my mouth. Mom had given me my choice of breakfast foods. I chose a waffle and eggs. Food had become just sustenance, even with as new as it was to not have everything turn to ice on the way down.

I had no idea what to do here, though. I didn't even know why Mom was obsessed with having me back. "You know, we shouldn't waste time. I've got a team to get back to. A mission to complete. What do you want?"

Wow, that came out harsh.

"I want you to be here with me."

That was it? No hidden motive? "I don't have time for this."

Drake cleared his throat. He had cleanly shaved this morning, so his face was bare, but his eyes were sure hairy at me. "Natalie said she'd contact you if anything comes up. She has my number. You have nothing but time to reacquaint with your mom."

Mom pushed her full plate away. She wasn't hungry. "Look, the house got blown up before I could tell you what I wanted to say. But I wanted to apologize, Laoni. I need to make it up to you. I want us to be a family. Live in the same house, breakfast every morning, dinner every evening, you go to school and graduate, have a future, know your sister."

I glanced at Gem, who gave me a soft smile. I really had no idea what her character was. I hadn't given it even an ounce of thought. Okay, fine, I had. But every single thought was how to kill her if she came after me, if she had Burner and Breather abilities combined.

Mom was breaking my heart, though she didn't know it. Future? For me? No way.

I did what I did best, though. I lied. "I'd like that, too."

Mom's face melted into relieved tears. "Good. I know you have a mission. How is that going, anyway?"

"Really amazingly well," Drake put in. "Your daughter is incredible."

Wow, real admiration from my stepdad. Cool, I guess. "Me and everyone else."

"And you," Redmond put in. I glared at him. So not helping.

"Look," I said and stood up. "This is nice and all. But I'm not used to sitting around. And you know you can't stay here. If it's your second house, the Breathers know it too."

Mom shook her head. "I bought it secretly under a false name."

I cast my gaze at Drake. "You know that's not enough."

He sighed. "Yeah, I know."

Lucky for them, I'd been on the run all my life. I knew what to do here. "Mom, I have to go back to my team. We need to plan for the next run. Once that's done, I think Scepter will think twice before coming after Burners again. It all lies on this. And as much as I'd like to get to know each other, being trapped together in one house isn't the best way to promote familial bonds. It might just kill one of us."

How little did they know how accurate that was. But I wasn't lying when I said I couldn't stay. Here, I was just waiting for death. Out there, I was fighting and waiting for death. Yeah. Okay, but it was better than watching the people love me who I'd have to leave behind.

Gem giggled. She didn't get how serious I was, but I still

gave her a smile. This was the first real interaction we'd had besides just that whole staring thing. I recognized her smile. It was mine. My heart ached. I couldn't leave them here. But I couldn't protect them either.

"So, what I'm proposing is that you and Drake and Gem go…" I wasn't so sure about this. I looked toward Mond. He gave me an encouraging nod.

"I really don't know how a human, Breather, and half of both will be welcomed in, but I want you to go to…" This was harder than I thought. I was revealing the secret of the Burners. The safe place where they didn't have to worry about Breathers. I was sending one to their side.

But I trusted him. I couldn't believe it, but I needed to. I had been given my mom back, the present I had wished for all my life. If she was going to remain safe, if my sister was going to, they needed the same protection as the Burners.

"There's an island that keeps Breathers away. It's a safe haven for Burners. There's a submarine that comes when we contact Nora. I've already asked Natalie to talk to her. She thinks you'll be welcomed."

Mom made a triangle out of her hands on the table. Her elbows reflected in the smooth surface. "You want us to run? To an island? Where we probably won't be welcomed? I don't think that's such a good idea."

I stopped her. "I do. If you trust me at all, know that you signed your death warrant as soon as you met up with me. Drake helped us liberate the Flyers. Scepter knows. You have become targets. It's not so comfortable to live with. And that was if your daughter didn't already have a target on her. I saw the info on her. They were waiting. When she turned sixteen, they would have dragged her away. But now? I know them. I've made my life knowing them. Please. I don't want you to end up like the Barclays."

Mom looked toward Drake. "What happened?"

He shook his head. "A tragedy. But it won't happen to us."

I gave a bark of laughter. "It *always* happens to me and anything I touch."

Mond gave me a look. He heard the judgment in my voice.

"Will you come get us? After it's over?" Mom asked. "Will we be a family?"

I stared at my reflection in the table. My black streak of hair. My eyes looked tired. My face wan, like a burnt-out light bulb. "Sure. We'll come home here where it's safe. I'll go to school. Maybe I'll test out of graduating or something. We'll have dinner every night."

I glanced at Mond, who wouldn't look back. He knew I was lying. Mom didn't. I wondered how cruel that was, to give her hope.

It didn't matter.

I gave Mom and Drake the information about where to meet up with the submarine, and they started packing. Mond disappeared to his room. This was too much for him. The future I was promising was killing him. He knew it was the worst lie I could ever say.

But if I had told the truth, I would have gotten more sad eyes, this time from my mom. Drake didn't know the truth. No one did except for Mond, Natalie, and me. Maybe Nora. That was what they had been whispering about so long ago. My death knell.

As Mom and Drake headed upstairs while Gem walked over to me. "Hi, we haven't even talked. Now I'm getting shipped off again."

I gestured to the living room. It was a wide sunken place with lots of homey throws and pillows on the long couches. Cinnamon-colored drapes cloaked the long windows. We both stood. We didn't touch each other, but I saw her hands fidgeting like she wanted to. I needed to explain stuff to her, somehow. If it really mattered. "I'm your sister."

"Yeah. But what happened? All Mom says is that she betrayed you. I hear them whispering about powers and such. I know…I'm supposed to have something, right? Mom says it will come. When did you…"

I saw the curiosity flowing out of her eyes. I wasn't just her sister. I was her answer key, the truth to her own abilities. How little she knew that she was something quite unique and unrepeatable.

"Gem, do you have any friends?" I asked instead.

She shook her head. "People at school think I have an attitude problem."

I grinned. We were so alike. "No one, then?"

Gem shook her head. "And now that we're here, and soon somewhere else, I doubt anyone will ever like me."

I slipped down to the couch and did something I didn't think I could. I pulled my younger sister to my shoulder and held her. "Gem, when you have a big thought, write it down. Sometimes, you can be your own best friend."

Gem blinked and looked up at me. Her round face looked so innocent, so unaware of what her abilities could bring her. "Okay, sure. Why not? But you're my friend, right? We're sisters. We're supposed to be friends."

I squeezed her hands between my own. "I wouldn't know."

"You do, too. Because I said so." Gem sounded so sure. Angry even. Yeah, she had an attitude, all right. Good. It might keep her alive.

"Yes, my sister. Anything you say, my sister." Then I attacked her belly with my fingers.

"Stop! I'm ticklish!" she screeched. Then she laughed so bubbly I couldn't actually believe this little ball of sunshine was my sister. I let her go and stared at her.

"You stay alive, you hear me. You just do it."

She took my orders seriously. "When we get back, I want to go everywhere with you," she decided.

My stomach churned. I pushed her away and got up. "We need to move faster. The submarine won't wait."

I escaped. I never had much to live for before. Just survival. If I had found out I had an expiration date when I was making a home in the sewers, planning on killing Farrell, I would have welcomed it. But now? I had Mond. I had Mom. Gem. And even Drake. And all my friends.

I didn't want to die.

And wouldn't you know it, this was when I would die. Life was a bitch.

CHAPTER 22

The sendoff was bigger than I thought it'd be. I was saying goodbye to my mom, again, Drake, and Gem. But Erin was saying goodbye as well, to her brother and sister. Tests had been done in my absence to see how far the Flyers had infected Butch and Carolyn.

Natalie had declared them free of foreign agents, but I did wonder how far she could figure that out with our limited supplies, stolen from here and there. Truth was, I think only a Flyer could tell if they were free.

It was a risk, to be sure, allowing a Bloodhound and two Flyers to go to our secret paradise. But it was necessary. There was no other place they'd be safe.

I stood on the shore and watched as the submarine disappeared under the water. Erin stood next to me. "You could go with them," I stated.

She gave me a sideways look. "You, too."

I almost laughed. But Erin had no clue what was going to happen to me. "I said it first. So that means you have to explain why not to me."

Erin swallowed. She looked older. I mean, in her eyes.

The rest of her was beautiful. Her crinkly black hair flowed well over her ears. But the maturity was in her eyes. I wondered if I was like that. Years seemed double living on the run. "I could say that I wanted to end this war so we could live happily ever after. But it'd be a lie. I want revenge."

I got it. "Good reason."

Erin's throat tightened. "They're gone. I didn't even get to say goodbye. I had them, and then I lost them."

I pursed my lips and pulled her close to me around the shoulders, trying to give some comfort. "I know. And now you'll have to continue. Each day. Each minute. It's tough. It never gets easier. But all I can say is keep them inside. Remember them."

Erin shook. Her eyes were dry. She was holding back her tears. "You were always so optimistic. I saw the darkness. But it's all darkness now."

We walked along, trying to catch up to the rest of the group. "You're made of fire. You make the light."

Erin spat roughly onto the sand, kicking the wetness as far as she could. "Nice. Are you making greeting cards now or something?"

I pulled her to a stop and looked into her eyes. "Erin, I know. Okay. We've been through it. Someday, remind me to tell you about the woman who died in front of me because I was stupid enough to take refuge in her home."

Erin's chin quivered. She was trying to stay strong. But while locked up in the facility, she never had to deal with what I had. I was *special*. "But if you let things like that dominate your mind, then you will have lost. The Breathers. Scepter. The ones against us. All of them will have won. Look to the light. Your brother and sister are alive. You have Cindy. You have a…future."

Erin cocked her head at that. She heard the hidden statement. I rushed to cover it up.

"Remember, everything is dark when hope is thrown out. Hope is the light that pushes away despair, okay? Keep it alive. Get your revenge but look to the future. One day, you can look at the Burners who have normal lives and say, 'Hey, I was a part of your liberation. I gave you your hope because I didn't give up mine.'"

Erin ran her fingers along her brow line. "Hey, Laoni, you'd make a great politician, you know. Changing people's minds when they're so firmly grounded."

"Erin!" I groaned.

"No. Sorry. I…You're right. I want to just fall apart. But I won't. I can't. But this future you're so sure of? I can't see it."

I smiled. It felt like a vice across my cheeks. "What else is new? You have been dark and cloudy as long as I can remember. Come on, it'll get better."

Erin's face crumpled. "I don't see how."

I didn't either. I pulled on her. "Let's go home. Our current home, anyway. We'll get your revenge."

Erin didn't smile, but she said nothing snarky either. Win! We reached the others.

~

The waiting time was the worst. Nothing was happening. No new information. My electricity was coming back bit by bit, faster than before.

I was bored. Though the new hideout was a lot more luxurious than the old swampy place, even it got very small when I walked it every day. Outside, it was a dull gray stone surrounded by a lake of water. Inside were three corridors, one leading out to a stony paradise with a waterfall tumbling down and a walkway looking over it. Inside were rooms stacked upon each other, a miniature, underground hotel with no windows. A huge room where we ate was to the left of the entrance.

The most disquieting thing about all of it was that it was so…different. I couldn't place my finger on it, but it hadn't been built for humans. The walls were a metallic green, but made of material I had never seen, while the endless lights required no electricity or power at all. They were dim, faded globes of green light, making the whole place seem like it was under the ocean instead of next to a lake.

I walked the hidden building under the dam more times than I could count. The little waterfall was my favorite place. It was loud enough to block my thoughts, but cozy enough to be comfortable. The smell was fantastic. Not at all moldy. It was a clean, fresh, water over a grassy and earthy smell.

Usually, I avoided all the others by going and staring at the waterfall, trying to make it freeze. Everyone else was settling in, making this place a home. We all got our own rooms. I think the others were just happy to get out of their prison and be away from the boring island. Bobby said how happy he was this place had computers. He was learning to fly a helicopter, of all things, just by reading guides and watching how-to videos. He could do it too. He was amazingly brilliant.

In fact, everyone but Erin was treating this new hideout as another facility—a new home. I couldn't. In addition to my secret death that was coming who knew when, I also hadn't been there when they were captured. I had failed at protecting them. Erin didn't want to see me because of her parents and siblings. I had no desire to see anyone myself. I stayed away.

Redmond found me on one of my many jaunts down to the waterfall. I was sparkling and throwing my lightning to make shapes. It wasn't going well.

"Beautiful," Mond said. "You're lit up again."

I nodded. "Can't help it. I'm living energy. The only way to get rid of it is to expel and shorten my life."

"Come on. Let's go and play some board games. It'll cheer you up."

I wanted to sink into him. But I'd do more than burn him now. I might cause him to meet his end like I was going to. And I wouldn't do that. Never. "No. I hate it here. I..."

Mond leaned against the thin railing. "It's better here than using up your energy too soon. Maybe it'd be best." He saw my face crumple. "What?"

"It's not. It's ugly here. Man-made. No nature except this waterfall, and even it's not natural. Made by the dam pushing the water into different places. Forced. I—"

"But you're alive to see it. That makes it good. You can be happy as long as life is in you."

That made me scream. My lightning shot upward, slipping harmlessly into the rock above me. "There's more to life than living! I don't even care that I'll die sooner than later."

Mond put his fists to his nose. I was hurting him. "How can you not care?"

"Because...I guess it seems fake." I calmed down and threw my lightning into the water. I lost some of my glow. "I've been in danger. Mortal danger. So close, I could have reached out and touched it. That feeling was intense. Scary. Almost exciting. This? No. It's far off. Unknown. Hidden somewhere in my skin. One day. Maybe next week. Tomorrow. Who cares? I can't accept it."

Mond reached out for me. I risked leaning on his shirt and staying away from his arms. "Then, if you don't care about death, what is it, Oni? Why are you so miserable?"

I pushed my face into his chest. His scent overwhelmed me. My senses went into overdrive. It was like I was next to him for the first time. Well, yeah. I had been avoiding him ever since my body lit up again.

"I miss my ice. I was just getting used to it. If I still had it, I would make sculptures. And the shapes I could have made out of this waterfall! I can't *do* anything. I want to create. To make shapes live. I don't know. It's stupid."

Mond tangled his fingers in my mane of hair, but he held his hand against my scalp. "It's not stupid. You're an artist who has no paint. An author who has no words. Makes complete sense to me. Oni…" His voice sounded subdued.

"Mond?" I asked.

"You ever think life is just a way to screw us up? That a being out there is getting some sick perverted pleasure out of seeing us suffer? I met you at a low time in my life. You made me feel alive. I finally saw some brightness in our future. And BAM!"

I jumped. His voice had risen loud enough to scream.

"You're going to be taken away from me. You can't create and are sad. I lost everybody. I'm going to lose you. Why? I just want to know why. It's like we're cursed. Or I am."

I thought about that. It did seem logical that some evil being out there wanted us to suffer. I thought about Erin. I knew what she would say.

"No. You're not cursed. Neither are we."

Mond's heart beat faster. He was so worked up in what he was saying. "How can you say that?"

"Because of our joy." I shot a thin line of electricity straight out away from us.

"No! What are you doing? You're draining yourself."

But I didn't stop until I was drained again. Another strand of my hair darkened.

"Why are you doing that?"

"Because of this." I kissed him. Our lips worked together to bring us the joy we'd had a few dozen times already and never got boring. If I could do this all day, I wouldn't miss my ice. I leaned my cheek into his.

"That is worth a million deaths," I said. "We've gotten a short time together, but it has given me more joy than I could have ever known. If the Breathers didn't exist, I would have traded that perfect life for this short moment with you."

Mond's jaw moved. He was grinning. He gave me featherlight kisses up my cheek and toward my eyebrows. "I've gotta say, you're right."

"Erin thinks I'd be a good politician."

Mond chuckled. "I don't know about that. But you sure made me see the light."

"It's true," I insisted. "Erin lost her parents, but at least she had some wonderful moments with them. Who can say which life is better? A boring one with no loss, or lots of loss mixed with lots of joy. How can you know what real happiness is if you haven't had real sadness?"

Mond held my head to his neck, desperately trying to keep me near him. Holding me past the inevitable fate I'd endure one day. "You are good, Oni. I can't stand…"

"No. You're right. Let's ignore it. I don't need to think about it every minute of every day. It's not here now. I'm living *now*. It's the future. No one put a date on my head. It could be ten years from this moment. Just…enjoy the present. Look not to the future."

Mond agreed. I could feel him fighting against it, but he did. I took my own advice and ignored my lack of ice. At least I was getting a handle on my new powers. If I was too hot to touch, all I had to do was get rid of it, and I could be almost normal. So what that it took my life? When it was gone, that was true living. Giving up a little energy to feel normal—worth it!

Of course, I was lit up again by the next week.

CHAPTER 23

Our mission had stalled, but something finally happened. No, it wasn't new information. Natalie called us all together into one room and looked grimmer than I had seen her for a long time. And that was saying something!

Everyone stayed far away from me. I could have easily killed any of them.

Bobby had made me a chair that didn't conduct electricity. My place of honor.

"So, what's up?" I asked as we all sat around the small room. Cindy had done her best to give it some personality. She had snuck out and gotten throw pillows galore, along with knitted blankets and thick rugs, all to keep us warm from the cold stone floor.

"Nothing," Natalie said.

Great! "Okay, so you just brought us all together for laughs?" I asked. My sizzling energy made noise in the small area. Crackling and spitting, waiting for something to destroy. Draining me slowly but surely.

"No. We have a mission." She tugged on the ends of her

hair as she sat on the edge of a chair made from wood with a soft cushion as the only padding. "It's just a two-person thing. The rest of you will have to wait here, be ready for a message. If we don't return, then the person who we put in charge has to figure out the next move."

Erin steepled her fingers. "Okay, so Laoni is staying here, the ipso facto leader while you're gone. But who's going with you?"

I wondered why she automatically assumed I wasn't the one going. I think everyone knew something was wrong with me by now. The fact that I couldn't shut off my powers, the ice that I no longer had. Everyone had asked me about it. I had smudged it over, telling them I was transforming. But not even the special clothing that made our powers stay in control helped me. I was a living light bulb.

That was, if anyone saw me at all. Though I was surrounded by people these days, I felt the same as when I was on the run. Alone. I couldn't tell them that someday, maybe soon, I'd permanently go out.

Then again, I think Erin might have guessed it. Why else would she be so ready to accept that I'd stay here?

"No. You're the leader," Natalie said to Erin. Erin's eyebrows rose. With a glance at me, I noticed Erin's question. Was that okay with me?

I had been the leader for a very long time. First, as the escapee from our prison, then as the glorified returning hero. No matter how much Erin was annoyed at me, she always looked to me to tell her what to do.

"Who's going?" Mond asked. He, too, seemed to think it was inevitable that I stayed here.

"Laoni and me. There's supposed to be a house where a Breather lives as a human. He should be able to lead us somewhere. Give us something to do. With a destroyed facility and two breeding grounds gone, he's needed. If we can get to his house and then follow him, we should find out where Scepter is or at least where he goes to report in. It could lead us out of this city or even out of this state. We may not make it back. Give us a month. Then run some recon missions yourselves. If you can find out anything, do it. If you have to, run. Nora will send out the submarine in two months for you to retreat if we haven't made it back in time."

Silence met that statement.

"Then Laoni and I will go," Mond said quickly. "Natalie, you have no skills left. I have mad skills."

Natalie shook her head. There was something to her eyes. Oh…She didn't expect to make it back. Who was this Breather we were going to scout out anyway?

"My orders are what I've said. Two people. That's it. You take over. Flee if you must. We have struck a huge blow. That's all we set out to do. Not win. Do as I say." She stood up and started shoving her hair into a ponytail. Maybe it was the hairstyle or maybe it was the fear in her eyes, but she looked younger than her years.

Mond objected, of course. "No way. If it's secrecy you're after, Laoni will destroy that in seconds flat. Look at her. Maybe we should all go. Kidnap the piece of…"

"No!" Natalie said. Ice coated her cheeks as she tried to get herself back under control. So, she wasn't out completely. "You have followed me, listened to me. You will do so again unless you want to fail."

Mond scoffed. He was ready to fight until death.

I quickly made ball lightning in my hands and spilled it all over until I was out. Then I sent it into my chair. "Mond, I trust Natalie. So should you. Besides…"

I let the heavy weight behind my words fall without a sound. He got it. He stared at me. I had known him for such a short time, but we communicated with our eyes.

"I don't want you to die."

"But I will."

"At least let me say goodbye."

"It's better if you don't see it. Say goodbye now."

No one else was privy to our secret communication. Natalie was more than surprised when Mond stomped out of the room but didn't offer any argument.

"Well, that's one. Anyone else have something to say?"

Cindy interrupted Erin. "Only that you have to return. Okay? No more deaths. We need victories now." She shot a sorrowful glance at Erin, who looked at her hands. She was still mourning her own loss.

"I agree," Erin said quietly. "No more."

How little they knew that I was a given!

"When do we leave?" I asked Natalie.

"An hour. We're taking the bus." Then she left the room, her arms swinging in angry bursts.

"Okay! What's up?" Bobby asked. It was funny how a year could change us all so much. His arms were like cannons. His blonde hair touched the edges of his massive shoulders. "It's like there's going to be a funeral."

Erin made a strangled cry and ran from the room.

"Way to go, Bobby," Cindy said with a glare at him and left too.

"What'd I say?" he asked.

"Erin's parents…You know they died."

"Oh." He looked at his hands. Two big packs of meat. "Yeah. I didn't realize. Everything happened so fast. We arrived. We were attacked. We were imprisoned again. It seems that's all life is. Who has time to mourn?"

I slid down to his seat and put an arm around his shoulders as much as I could. "You miss the island, don't you?"

"Not the boring emptiness with no real way of learning

anything. But, kind of. It was simpler. And the bugs were amazing."

I laughed and hit his chest. "Ah, Bobby, you don't change."

His teeth showed. Perfect white. "Bugs are easier to understand than people. I've never done well. I admired you and your attitude. Hey, what's up with your powers anyway? I feel…"

"Don't!" I snapped. "Just…"

He didn't back down. "But is that going to happen to the rest of us? Or is it just you? And when does it end? How does it feel?"

I cuffed his head affectionately. "Bobby, stick to analyzing bugs."

"No. Really. How is this all going to end? I thought it'd be a happy ending. It was, but then time goes on. Is any happy ending really an ending? Or do you wait long enough for the bad ending?" His shoulders hunched down, and he was still amazingly big.

"Oh, Bobby. It's always a bad ending when you stop living no matter how old you are. I gotta go. Mond is waiting for me. I have to tell him goodbye and then get to work." I stood up.

Bobby stared at me. "Come back, okay? I don't want to know what it's like to mourn someone. I don't want to walk around like Erin does. I don't want half my life to be shaded."

Bobby was the most innocent of all of us. From the moment he arrived at our facility, he missed no one. I wondered where he came from. Was he kidnapped? Or was he sold?

"Bobby, we haven't talked much."

He shook his head. "We used to all the time. You listened to all my talk about bugs. You told me what you found out about grammar, and words, and languages. Then you left. You came back and saved us all. But there's no time to talk."

I turned and ran away. I can't even say why I did that. Maybe because Bobby nailed it down better than anyone else could have. I was dying. I didn't know when. But it'd be soon if my flare-ups were any indication. And I'd never talk to Bobby again.

I had once left all of them. Running until I grew up while they had stayed inside the facility. Living, talking, being. I felt as if I had stopped until Mond showed up. Then time, as tricky as it was, moved again. I found my friends again.

But I had never really stopped to *feel*. To understand what it was I was missing before I even did. All my diary entries, and I still didn't understand *me*.

I met Mond by the waterfall, where we had talked earlier.

"It's a suicide mission," he said when he saw my face. "That's why Natalie isn't taking anyone else. She thinks she's expendable, and you're dying anyway."

What else could I say? I grabbed his collar and kissed him hard, putting all my passion into it. He returned the kiss. I could feel his heart pouring into mine.

"Oh, Mond," I gasped and pulled away. "Come on! You knew this was coming."

"I liked lying, okay? But when Natalie…" His fingers walked down my shirt, hitching at the end of my sleeve. His fingers stroked the inside of my wrist. "It's all over. There's no way out."

"It was over as soon as I stepped into the machine." I leaned our bodies against the railing, letting the spray hit my cheek. The sound of the waterfall pounded into my ears. "You saved me. Gave me so much more time. Gave us a moment."

Mond's eyes were shiny gray marbles filled with unshed tears and lost tomorrows. "A moment?"

"Let's face it, all we Burners have are moments. It's more than a lot of others get. What we live now? It's more than an old friend of mine had. Belinda."

Mond nodded. "You've mentioned her a few times."

"Died by the machine at only sixteen. She lived so well. But she's gone now. We have more. And…" I held my breath as I pulled my latest diary out from under my shirt. It was a dingy gray. I got my notebooks when I could. Though I wished I had a more decorated one, with scrolls of gold or something.

"What is this?" he asked. He knew exactly what it was.

"Me. Read it. All of it. The rest are in my backpack. I want you to read them. You can see who I am and what I wanted, desired. Even if I don't make it back, you can still have me. You'll have all of my moments."

Mond made a guttural cry that didn't sound human.

I shoved my diary into his hands. "Read it. Read me. I love you." I kissed him again, pressing my diary into his chest.

Then I escaped through the door and down the long hallway.

~

I stared at the passing scenery. It was funny that no matter where I went, highways seemed to always be the same. Unending roads going to destinations I really didn't want to go to.

Natalie hadn't said much since we started this journey. We were both consumed with the stuff in our own heads, I guess. I kept seeing Mond's eyes, wondering if I'd return. Knowing that even if I did, it wouldn't be for long.

"You hungry?" Natalie asked. I blinked and turned toward her.

"Not really."

"Regardless, I'm stopping."

I rolled my eyes. Natalie wasn't the best company right now. We had a strange relationship at best. Sometimes she acted like my mother. Others she was my friend. But she was downright impossible on this trip.

"How much longer until we get there?" I asked.

Natalie shook her head.

"What?" I asked.

"It's just funny that after all you've been through, you're still asking, 'are we there yet?'" She signaled she was going to take the off-ramp, her eyes scanning the road for cars to avoid accidents and Breathers. You know, certain death. It didn't take long before she went through the drive-through, got some inedible food, and we were off again.

Then the silence began again. Finally, I couldn't take it. At first, I had been glad of the quiet she afforded me. But it only made me think of Mond. I had wanted a mission like this just to *stop* thinking. So far, we were only driving.

"Okay, so spill!" I announced.

Natalie finished off her bite with a grimace. "I can't believe people eat this on a regular basis," she muttered.

I tried not to get distracted. She was changing the subject. "Not everything can be good. Makes me wish for when I ate only ice. It might be preferable now." I shoved the wrappings back into the bag and tapped the dashboard. "Natalie…"

"What?" she asked. The sun was in her eyes, so she pulled down the sun visor.

"I think it's important to know all your issues before we go into potential battle together. So far, you've been giving the orders, staying away from the action. Now, we're supposed to fight together against someone who is a big danger. I need to know what's wrong."

"Well…Hmm. How can I explain? You've met a few nasty Breathers. They range from bad to worse."

"And good, like Drake," I pointed out. My fingers moved to play with the window opener.

Natalie shook her head so hard it sounded like her bones were breaking. "No. He is a rarity. Incredible and insane, but true. I have never seen someone like him. And even now, I have Nora keeping close tabs on him. The point is, there are some creepy ones and then there are the ones you wouldn't be satisfied to just kill. You'd want to torture them first. Bru'G-un is one of the latter."

I wrinkled my nose. So far, Breathers had had names that I recognized. This one didn't seem to be like Paul, or Farrell, or Digory. "Who is it?"

"A Rider. One that has been here since the beginning. I've met him in my travels. Almost got killed by him in the past." Natalie suddenly slammed the wheel with both her fists.

"Okay," I said, watching the bus fishtail a bit. There were very few drivers on the road around us. No cops. Good. "But you're upset about more than him. You've been upset. Is it Erin? And her…"

"Just say it!" Natalie yelled, speeding up. "I got them killed. I should have known the Breathers would still be tailing all families that had a Burner in them. But stupid me! I thought they had given up on that. I thought we were safe!"

The bus shook with the speed Natalie was forcing it to. "Oh, come on, Natalie," I said. "How could you have possibly known?"

"If I were a better person, I would have known *she* wouldn't let anyone go. Not even one person. And knowing that your sister was still watched, that a Breather was in the house with her and that was the only reason they ignored her…I should have hidden better. I got them killed. Erin's eyes when she looks at me…"

"Umm, maybe you should slow down," I said, looking behind us. Was it my imagination, or was there a police car behind us?

"I'm failing! I have tried since I found out what I was to save people." Natalie wasn't listening to me. "I should have known!"

"Natalie! The cop!"

She flashed her eyes in the rearview mirror, glaring at the lights. "Can't they see we're on a mission? I'm going on a diatribe against myself here!" She sped up even more.

"Natalie, what do we do? I know you can't prove this is yours. Do you even have a license?"

Natalie hissed.

Great. It was up to me. This was actually beyond scary. To have the one person I looked up to most losing it made my own grasp on reality suffer a bit. What was worse was that I had to attack a human to get us out of it. Any more time, and the cop would call for backup. We so didn't need *that*!

I climbed into the back and stared at the cop car. Ah, electric. Good. I zapped one solitary line into his car. No matter how much I expelled recently, I felt it all there, ready for use. I was indefatigable.

Electricity wriggled throughout the car and shut off the whole system. I didn't think the cop was hurt. The car just slowed down. I quickly climbed back in front and gestured to a nearby exit. "Pull off. *Now!*"

Natalie grimaced but listened. She was ahead of me, though. She did a quick U-turn down a nearby street and then we rumbled around until she yanked the wheel to pull into a large yard with a few trees in it. She parked behind one and let her head fall on the wheel.

"Sorry," she muttered. "I know. I know. I just…Leave me alone. No, I do *not* want to switch places. Like you could do better. Just drop it."

Somehow, I didn't think she was talking to me. For one, she made no sense. And two, she was muttering under her breath, her eyes far off and glassy.

"This is more than just guilt," I said when she finally rolled her head to look at me. Embarrassment burned her to her ears.

"Yeah. It is."

"You know. You know who *she* is."

Natalie sighed deeply, so mournful it made my teeth hurt. "Yes. I do."

"And this Rider, Bru'G-un. He's part of it."

Natalie pinched her top lip between her fingers and held them there. "Bru'G-un is my sister's lover…"

It felt like she slapped me. I had just gotten associated with the whole sister thing. Gem was wonderful. A mystery that I wanted to solve. I looked forward…Well, I *would have* looked forward to when this was all over and I could have gotten to know her. I knew Nora, how close she and Natalie were. They had a psychic connection that baffled even me with the two sets of powers I've had in my life. To think Nora had been with a Rider. Oh, eww, barf. Gag me with a steam shovel.

"Not Nora." Natalie knew what I was thinking.

I breathed a huge sigh of relief. Then I threw my hands up in the air. "Then you have another sister?"

"Our older sister. Molly Larson. She's…I've lied to you. To all of you. You ever wonder what made Nora and me so ready to save Burners? Why we didn't just save ourselves and move on?" Natalie didn't look at me. She just kept pinching her lip and looking at the quiet house in front of us. Somewhere in the distance, sirens were roaring, coming closer and then fading away again. We were unseen.

"You're kind and caring." I wasn't ready for this. A slimy chill was creeping up my back.

"No. We were selfish. When we found out we had powers, we used them to steal, sneak around. Our parents grounded us so often, it made our heads spin. If anyone crossed us at school, they were frozen. Mom and Dad kept moving us around. Molly resented us. She already did because we were twins and had a special connection she wasn't part of."

I was puzzled over all this. My own experience had been one of rejection. Natalie's parents sounded more open-minded.

"Okay…I'm trying to understand how Molly is relevant other than having *really* bad taste in boyfriends." I could feel my power buzzing, wondering when I'd light up again.

"Molly is Scepter."

Ouch. A swift punch. No gloves on. I got it. "She created it all because she wanted revenge on you."

Natalie nodded. "I don't know how, but she started searching for ways to…"

"Kill you?" I asked.

"No. Get our powers. She was too jealous. She wanted ice. She wanted to rule. She said over and over again how unfair it was that two idiots like us had gotten powers that she would have been able to actually use. She could change the world, she said. Make it into a better place. She was always intelligent. She turned toward any rumors, myths, and out-and-out lies to find any way she could be like us."

I closed my eyes. "The machine."

"She found Riders. I don't know where they came from. But they've been on Earth for a very long time, in secret, obviously. I don't know if they're a hidden invasion or what. But they hate Burners too."

I couldn't take this all in. Natalie's sister, Molly, was Scepter. She had created the machines with some aliens' help. "But…why didn't you tell us?"

"I was too ashamed. I stopped calling her sister twenty years ago. I had no idea how far her ambition went. Nora and I set up the island for people to escape her. But Molly won't be happy until she has eradicated all of us. And now this Better Suit? I had no idea she would actually do this."

I pushed my head against the headrest, trying to get the tension out of my neck. "What does this suit do?"

"I'm not sure. But my guess is that Molly would make it so it could fight any Burner. With Rider's tech and energy from Burners…I'm afraid she can easily kill us if we took her on one-on-one. And this?"

Natalie clapped her hands together and suddenly, her skin changed to pure ice. Inch by inch under her clothing, her skin solidified, throwing off vapor in the heat of the car. Her hair froze solid, strand by strand, until it was just icicles.

"The best I can do against my sister, and yet she had the power to eradicate all of us. She has slipped into everywhere. She even has spies on humans I wouldn't have thought of. She is always one step ahead of me."

I gaped. Natalie was so utterly *beautiful* right now. Pure icy perfection. Even I, another Burner, couldn't fight against her beauty. "How are you doing that?"

"I didn't tell you what happens to an old Burner. They can complete a transformation into their element. But it's dangerous for me. It takes my energy faster than I can know."

I immediately thought of Mond. "Mond? Will he be able to become a man of fire?"

Natalie surprised us both by bursting out into a laugh.

"Okay, I forgot how it is to be in love. Your first question would be that. Not about you. Not about what my sister is. No. How is Mond going to be? It's so darned cute!"

I worked very hard not to slap her. "I know I'm a lost cause! I'm like lightning now. And besides, I'll die before I get old enough. Whatever. Okay, fine. Stop!"

Natalie pulled her icy lips to a grimace again. Then she smacked them together and became human again. Or at least not ice.

"So, what's up with this Rider?"

"He's our direct connection with Molly." Natalie was deathly serious now. "We go after him, we find her. And that's who we're going after. We're going to kill her."

CHAPTER 25

REDMOND

*L*aoni,

I've read your diaries. They're five stars! I simply couldn't put them down! Ha ha. All joking aside, I miss you. I never knew all your hidden thoughts. To think you're still talking to me even when you're not here...

And soon that's all I'll have. So, let me tell you what I'm feeling. You gave me a record of you. I don't even know how to reciprocate except to write down everything I feel and hope that one day I can give you back your own diary and let you read me.

You've been gone a week. Erin's become totally obsessed with leading all of us. But let me tell you, she's no you. I'd follow you to the ends of the Earth.

It feels as if we've had our ears cut off. We have no clue what to do or where to go. Natalie and Nora had been the ones to listen to. They knew stuff. Found out junk. Now, Erin sends a few of us out to gather info. All we can figure out is that there are very few Breathers around here.

Not that we're looking hard, Laoni. You know the rules better than all of us. They catch our scent, they follow us to our hideout.

Oh, yes! Speaking of which. We actually found out more about where we're living. You'll never believe it. I'm not sure I do. You see...Wow, writing this truth stuff is hard. I was going to lie and say I accidentally found an old diary—yeah, a whole lot of diary reading going on, let me tell ya. But the truth?

Laoni, I was going insane. I felt like if I didn't burn something every single day, I would explode. You were inside my skin, and when you were not around me, I felt itchy. Burny, if that's a word. I wanted to look strong. Like, hey, I don't need nobody!

But here it is. Truth. I need you. And I can't function without you. I want to scream and burn and fly and run and scream some more. I want to punch something! I do. I have been the one to find a lot of the Breathers recently.

Their faces meet my fists. They go out. I am so damned angry! I hate the world. I hate everybody. You were here. Now you're gone. I'm weak. Don't tell anyone, Laoni.

I'll get back on topic now. It just feels really good to admit this to someone. I still feel my heart beating like a hammer against my ribs, but at least I've admitted it.

Okay, so this hideout. Oni! I found a diary when I tore apart a wall with my fire. I used it like a drill. I burned through that sucker like a hot knife through butter. You should have seen it!

You would have been very proud of your guy. I hope. Or maybe you would have been freaked out by my screams of rage. Yeah. I'm a bit freaked out myself, to be honest. I tried to keep it in. Since Dad died. Since those people burst into flames. Since I was thrown from the car and watched as innocents screamed in fiery deaths. Okay, get it together, Redmond.

But I noticed that there was a secret room. A hidden area completely hidden. When I explored, I noticed that in one of the rooms, there was a switch that opened the door. I wouldn't have had to burn it so utterly from the other side if I had found it.

Cindy let me have an earful for being in her room until I pointed out the hidden area. I swear that girl can punch!

So, we opened a secret room. It was cool. Yeah, I'm no writer,

Oni. Gotta be honest. This stuff is hard! But anyway, there was a hidden area of files. I have no clue where it came from. But we have a whole lot of time waiting. So, I read the diary of the man who came before.

Or should I say...alien! Dun, dun, dun! Yeah, seriously. An alien came to Earth in the sixties. According to the diary, he was waiting for an invasion, trying his best to save Earth. At first, I thought I was reading a science fiction book, but all of it coincided with real dates in history. Real stuff happening. This place was his secret base with a handful of other freedom fighters. Their previous world was taken over by these creeps, and they destroyed any natural resource. When those jerks had used up enough of their own planet, they decided they wanted to take over other's.

This dude, name of Te'rGar, had his army come here first and started to use their advanced technology to...Okay, here's where it gets complicated—and utterly exciting! He knew about DNA manipulation. He was putting everyone here through tests and sticking them in machines to get them going.

I have no idea what his ultimate goal was. I don't even know if he was a quote-unquote good guy. If he had his friends' approval for all these experiments or not.

It's all incomplete. Which sucks. I can't just wait for the sequel. This place was discovered. All the records were hidden, but let me just copy down the last paragraph of his, so you can see where he left off.

"I will finish writing in my new home world's language this journal. My last of all journals. They have found us. I intend to go out fighting. I have enough modifications to make it hard for them, even with all their technology. I have previously in my life said my farewells to everyone I ever loved, so death is my next great greeting.

"This new planet has physics I don't understand. Fire and ice, extremes of temperature that even they don't understand.

"Let them come.

"I await them."

Pretty interesting, huh? If it weren't for that last bit, I'd just think it a cool story. But, Oni, I'm getting a chill down my spine. We just happened to find a place where aliens talk about the elements? Where someone with "technology" is coming to destroy them?

If I didn't know better, I'd say Te'rGar was a Burner and the people coming were Riders. Drake did say that the Riders were aliens. Could it be?

Could Te'rGar have had something to do with all of this?

I can see your face now, giving me that special smile you reserve for me. You're skeptical, I know! If you were here, I'd debate you. But you're not here.

I don't know where you are. I can't even begin to imagine you're okay. It's driving me crazy. Of course, crazy is such an inadequate word for what I am.

Damn it! I need a distraction. Anything!

I can't even live through a week without you. How am I supposed to make it through the rest of my life?

Why is it I only write in this thing when I'm worried you're going to die? This sucks cheese!

I just had an idea. No one else cares if I'm here or not. I've never been much of a group person. I'm going to find out what happened to Te'rGar. If you were here, you'd be against it. Your eyes would light up with frustration about me doing something "stupid."

But, sweet Oni, you aren't here, so I'm free to be stupid. Dear, darling, lover. Hmm, I remember you hate me calling you endearments. Again, you aren't here. You may already be dead.

Excuse me.

I'm back. I had to burn my blankets to a crisp. I can't contain my anger at everything.

Look, Oni, I want you to read this someday, but I bet you won't. I've got this funny feeling in the pit of my stomach that tells me you're not going to be here much longer. You're slipping through my fingers. And as I grasp tighter and tighter, the more you slip.

So, I'm going to risk myself. I'm going to be reckless. I'm going to burn everything until I have something to do. And since there is a really cool mystery here, I'm going after it.

How, you ask? By following a trail backward. The guy, Te'r-Gar, mentioned that he bought equipment on Earth. He used our tech to make new tech. Maybe melded it with his own, but he left a trail. Paper or otherwise. I'm going to find the person or corporation and I'm going to make them tell me what they know.

The way I see it, Te'rGar had more than just his allies around. He died ten years after he started up here. That's a lot of time to be invisible. There is someone alive today who remembers him, I just know it.

It's probably stupid. A waste of time. But I have way too much time right now. Too much time causes too many worries. Too many people asking if I'm okay. Too many lectures. "Redmond, calm down." "Redmond, she'll be fine." Blah, blah, blah!

You won't be fine, even if you come back. I'd do anything to save you. I can't. So, let's waste some time!

I'm bringing the diary with me. I'm bringing you with me. I'm gonna do what you would do if you were here and not off dying. Write about my mission. And too bad if you disagree, Oni. Because I'd rather die than have that future where I have another girl. Children. A life without you. Hell, that's what it would be.

No. I'm on a quest of my own. I'm going to find Te'rGar's trail or die trying. Well, gotta sneak out so no one will ask me where I'm going.

Signing out.

CHAPTER 26

Okay, turns out that finding someone is harder than running! Natalie had led us to this house, but what had we done for a week? Watched a stupid Rider live his stupid life.

I had never wondered, never cared, what a Rider did on a daily basis. I mean, I knew that I had been captured by one, and that monster had owned a house. But to watch a Rider go to work, come home, watch hours of television, and go to the bathroom before bed? It was ridiculously dull!

We had parked our bus about a block down on an empty enough side street with our old friends the trees blocking us from view or scent. Natalie had brought computerized binoculars with heat sensors. We had snuck in while he was gone and put in some bugs so we could hear any conversation. And we sat and waited. Reading. Talking.

I learned more about Natalie's life and how this whole thing started. I still couldn't believe that Natalie was a part of something that was already there. After Molly had betrayed them, Natalie and Nora had dedicated their lives to stopping their sister. But the only real power they had was to save themselves. Molly had already gone beyond them by the time they found out.

"Yeah, I want a pizza. Pepperoni. Double cheese."

The voice annoyed me. The Rider was ordering dinner.

"It's amazing he's not five hundred pounds. Isn't that his fifth pizza in the last three days?" I asked, flicking the seat I sat on. One seat had been pulled out to make room for the spying equipment. All the windows had been blackened with window tint.

"It's not fair," Natalie agreed. "They get to eat whatever they want and never gain."

I went back to my book. During the day, we didn't have much to do, because the Rider—AKA Fred Smith—played well as a human. He was a parking lot attendant. He obviously received a lot of money from Molly, though, so why he worked made no sense to me. Maybe to keep his secret identity better. He had neighbors. They'd probably wonder sooner or later if he didn't go to work.

But the very nature of Bru'G-un's work made it impossible to stay hidden. There were few parking spots for us to use, and sooner or later, we'd draw attention to ourselves.

Besides, it was painfully dull watching him sit and play with his phone all day. Natalie and I agreed he wouldn't be making any rendezvous with Molly in a parking lot.

So, we waited near his house.

His phone beeped, and finally the words we'd waited for came along. "Molly! How long do I have to wait to see you? I miss you."

I stuck my finger down my throat, and Natalie nodded, mimicking me.

Then the Rider's tone turned serious. "That many? This is ridiculous. The Burners aren't even a threat."

I smirked. Yeah, really?

"Okay. Yeah. Makes sense. Don't you worry your pretty little head about it. Breathers are easily made. We can bring them back. Flyers are almost a liability thanks to the side of them that isn't controlled. We just need to kill this group."

Silence.

"Molly, we can't throw that many into the machines, which means we'd have to imprison them, which means they could possibly do what they did at Paul's facility."

He was quiet. "Yes, baby, I'm sorry. I know. I know. We'll capture them. You can personally watch each one go into the machine. How much longer before your suit is…Well, that's wonderful news. So, then why all the extra energy? There's no need for that much more money. Once we get rid of this group, you'll be free to get any Burner that shows up. Kill one faction and the rest won't ever dare again, right?"

Again, a beat.

"I know. I'm sorry, baby. We'll get them. Can I see you? I'd like to see this Better Suit and what it can do."

Natalie and I stared at each other, holding our breaths. Was this finally it? Would our week of surveillance pay off?

"Yes! An amusement park?" Bru'G-un said. "Strange place. Oh, it's abandoned. Okay. Plenty of space to check out your new suit. Good. I'll see you there."

Natalie jumped into the front seat and I buckled up. He was leaving now. Natalie pulled around the corner, and we watched as his garage door opened. Out came his sleek black motorcycle with extra rims and chrome all over everything. The handlebars were extra big to fit his meaty hands. He was off.

And we followed. Natalie watched him, checked his turns before following. She bit her lip as she watched him speed up.

"Laoni, hold the wheel."

I did so. Natalie bit her lips in concentration, holding her thumb and forefinger an inch apart. I had no clue what she was doing, but the bike was getting away.

"Natalie…" I urged. The bus was slowing down. We were going to lose him!

"Shhhhhh!" Natalie hissed and an arrow-shaped ice cube popped out of her fingers. She opened the window and shot it through the air. It sped so fast, I couldn't see it, but it didn't matter. The bike was gone. The weeklong stakeout was useless. We couldn't follow him.

"Natalie…" My eyes widened as she slumped over the wheel.

"Nat! No. Come on!" The bus slowed, and I quickly turned it off. Sitting in the middle of the road.

She pushed her eyes open and waved at me to calm down. "I'm okay. An ice tracer just takes too much out of me."

"What?" I asked with my mouth hanging open.

Natalie turned the bus back on and swallowed a few times. "Well, yeah. It has to constantly communicate with my brain where he is. That's a lot of energy."

I stared at her. "Ice tracer? You can trace someone?"

She nodded. She looked exhausted. "Just gotta follow its signal now. Laoni, there's so much you don't know about our powers."

I just pointed at the road. "Drive. We need to meet up with Molly and that Better Suit." I so didn't want to know about everything I'd miss. I'd lost my ice. I lost everything. Soon, I'd lose my life.

"What do you think this Better Suit is?" I asked again. I hadn't let up much on that question.

"No reason to speculate," Natalie said with a bit of venom seeping out of her voice. "We'll see soon. You'd better get fired up for action, Laoni. We're going in blazing. That Rider isn't one to play around. And my sister…"

I heard it in her voice. The betrayal. The anguish that someone that should have been such an ally was an enemy.

"Do *not* underestimate her, ever."

I agreed. As we rumbled down the streets, I wondered what city we had finally ended up in. There were so many places that looked identical in this world.

The amusement park the Rider mentioned was far out of town. Smack dab in a lot of trees. Rundown and forgotten. I'm not sure it had ever even opened for business. There were no signs, just old rides.

I saw a few rollercoasters flash between the trees. Only our bus was on the solitary road leading to it, overgrown and lined by a broken fence with graffiti on it.

Natalie found a nice copse of trees to hide our bus behind, and we hoofed it the rest of the way.

I saw the recent tracks of the bike that went in, tearing the grass apart, smashing everything in its way. We walked under a huge archway that used to have lights on it. All the light bulbs were broken. The grass crunched under my feet. The smell of old buildings mixed with nature sent a rusty essence into my nose.

"You ready?" Natalie asked.

I nodded.

She shook her head, and then icy hair fell down. She looked at me with eyes perfectly sketched in ice. Frigid eyebrows. Her clothing was the only thing not cold and see-through.

"I'm looking forward to seeing my sister," Natalie said. "It has really been too long."

Ouch. I'd hate to have that tone directed at me. I wriggled, and all my energy came over me again. I lit up and sparkled in the dry air. The grass plumed into smoke at my feet. The smell burned my nose.

Natalie and I punched fists and walked in. In this state, my electricity did nothing to her.

It was time to fight.

CHAPTER 27

The creepiest place in the world has to be an amusement park meant for laughter and joy reduced to a graveyard. Empty rides. Gigantic painted faces. Empty, barren grounds overrun with grass.

The feeling of ghostly figures that were supposed to be here.

To be looking for a Rider and a person who was the mastermind behind all my suffering through this world of dead laughs? That made my hair rise on end.

"Any sign of them?" I asked.

Natalie glared around the huge area, flashing from one place to the other. Even the Rider's motorcycle wasn't in view.

"This isn't good," Natalie pointed out. "They have no reason to hide."

We stood back-to-back. Even with my sparkling lightning and Natalie's ice form, I felt weak. Small. Defenseless.

So many eyes were on me. Out of every shadow, a person could appear. It was deathly quiet. Not even the roar of the Rider's motorcycle could be heard.

"Is there a way we can sneak up on them if they could be anywhere?" I asked.

Natalie shook her head. "Molly! It's your wonderful younger sister come to call!" she yelled out. There was a flutter of birds nearby, but then the roar of what I was expecting came.

The Rider came flying out of a gap, aiming for me.

Stupid.

I lashed my arm out, spilling lightning into him. I hooked an end and picked him up.

Oh, yeah! Who had the power now?

I wiggled him around, zipping him into the ground and then pulling his struggling body about ten feet into the air next to me. "Hello," I said sweetly. "Name's Laoni. Can you remember that?"

Bru'G-un snapped his wrist and tentacles came out, slapping me in the face.

I dropped him with surprise, then he whistled and the motorcycle he was riding came roaring forward. I shot lightning at it.

"Move!" Natalie yelled and took the bike's charge straight on. It crumpled into her ice. The Rider got painfully to his feet. His face seemed so human. If it weren't for the tentacle a minute ago, I'd still think he was.

The Riders weren't nearly as attractive as everyone else. This one had a big face, round like a moon, big massive shoulders the size of an ox, a muted red vest over thick black pants, and a wide belt with one silver circle on it. His eyes were pale, almost white, not purple like the Breathers. Funny how I once thought that the Riders were of the same category. They went well beyond.

Aliens, Drake had said.

Bru'G-un whistled for his bike again, and it moved back to him where, he mounted it. A grinding sound was heard, and the motorcycle transformed, slipping upward to almost become a part of his body. The wheels were on his feet, and he held the handlebars in his fists.

"It's a pleasure," he announced. "I had no idea I was being followed. You're good."

Natalie stood next to me. She was spinning around, looking for Molly. Where was she? If the Rider didn't know about us, then Molly had to. She was watching us.

"I have to say, as I look at the two of you, I see what kind of weapon Burners are. But you still have weak, thin skin, so easily torn." He twisted the handlebars and two missiles shot out. I picked them out of the air. So easy. Getting easier every minute.

I lifted into the air, floating over the ground. "This is the man who's so scary to you?" I said to Natalie. This was incredible. It was the first time I had ever felt overpowered against a Breather—a Rider, I mean. So very different.

I didn't have to run and hide. I slammed my power into his face.

His whole mutant bike went over, smashing him into the ground.

"What did he do to you?" I asked, feeling an evil spark. I knew what one had done to me, or almost had. I remembered killing him. Funny. I didn't care as much as I used to. "Did he hit you?"

Natalie looked at me with confusion. She wasn't judgmental. But she didn't know what game I was playing at. And she still was looking for Molly.

Me, I didn't care. Let her come. Along with her Better Suit. I was invincible.

I zipped across the air to come face to face with Bru'G-un. "See," I said conversationally. "I don't know what you did. But I can guess."

I lit up my hand to a flaming pillar of a fist and slammed

it into his face. This was for all the moments I felt weak. For all the times when I ran, terrified I wouldn't see morning. For the humans who had gotten in the way.

For my whole life!

I zapped into the air and lifted him up. Shaking him, I looked toward Natalie. "This pathetic thing was what you were afraid of!"

Gloating, I spun around in the air and tossed him and his bike in the same movement. I heard his heavy body slam into the railings of the roller coaster. It fell in a shower of dust and rust.

"Laoni!" Natalie scolded.

"What?" I demanded. "Am I having too much fun?"

"No," a new voice said. "You're wasting too much energy. Leaving you nothing to deal with me."

Out of nowhere, a heavy blow threw me. I flew until I hit the ground, shoving dust and debris up as my head went into the wall of a Ferris wheel. It was like a truck had hit me. Lucky for me, I had so much electricity up. Almost a protective barrier.

I shook my head to clear my eyesight, but all I saw was a grinning face as I was shoved further into the wall, pounding me against the wood until the whole thing came down. I was buried.

Outside I heard Natalie. "Molly! No. You stop it right now."

Molly gave a derisive laugh.

I struggled through the tight feeling. I was buried. Metal and wood twisted around me, giving me an unnatural hug.

"Nice suit, isn't it?" Molly said. She had the same accent as Natalie, but hers was rough, filed down with venom and rage. "I was wondering what would happen if I came against another Burner. And she was an Alternate Burner too! Wow, how pathetic."

I heard a whooshing noise, and then the sound I didn't want to hear. Natalie was choking.

"Ah, little sister, did you come to kill me? I hope Nora can feel your pain as I choke the life out of you."

Then the sound of ice cracking.

No!

I pushed all the debris away from me, exploding in a lighted ball of rage. I jumped up into the sky to see what I had feared. Molly was there in her Better Suit. But it was huge! A machine with whirring parts and lots of spinning gears to show off the unnatural form of it.

It was designed to look like a suit jacket and pants but failed miserably. The arms were more like humanoid motorcycles, round with mechanical fingers at the end. She was in the center, almost like wearing it, but she was in a cabin of buttons and levers. She was under a pretty glass dome that was attached to the suit. The sleeves were formed into guns around the big metallic fists. One hand had its fingers around Natalie's throat, squeezing her, showing the cracks in the ice.

Molly wasn't nearly as attractive as Natalie or Nora, but I think it was mainly her expression. The ugly sneer that reached her eyes. The same blonde hair was on her head, but it was flat against her skull, far from the Burners' beauty.

"Let her go!" I screamed and shot through the wrist. It dropped Natalie. *Great!*

I got slammed from behind. A missile loosed from the suit ripped through my electricity and punched me. I held my ground, well, air and spun around to go at her again.

"You?" she demanded. "You're the one giving me so many problems?"

"You?" I mocked. "You're the idiot who made my life a living hell?"

I slammed her again, but she absorbed the energy easily.

The suit protected her. She floated through the air, aiming. I dove downward as she loosed six projectiles at me.

Bam, bam, whizz! Whistling past my ears. I went on my back in the sky and made a hook and slammed it into anything I could reach on the suit. Then I whipped her through the air, aiming at any structure I could find. To knock her out. To break her suit.

To my surprise, she stopped, and suddenly the top of her suit shot ice at me while the bottom shot fire.

All that energy stolen from Burners!

It knocked me out of the sky. Once again, I traveled across the ground, slamming against rocks and rubble. My skin tore and bled.

"Laoni!" Natalie yelled. She rushed over to me, and we watched Molly laughing in the sky. "You're sparkling in and out."

"No energy. Wasted it." I gave a shaky grin. "Where's the Rider?"

Before she could answer, Molly pulled Natalie into the sky, and once again, her hand crushed her throat. "I want some ice cubes. You can cool my drink, sis." She sneered.

My arms were clamped suddenly. The Rider was behind me. Away from his motorcycle, his big hands were squeezing my arms. "Hiya, sweetie. You had fun with me. I look forward to having my fun with you."

I did the logical thing and lit up. He burst off my body. I flew up again. I zapped Molly's suit at least six times, but this time, her hand wasn't stopping. The hand I had ripped off was back on, reattached and choking the life out of Natalie. Her ice went in and out.

"Leave her alone!" I screamed.

"No," Molly said. "I've dreamed of this moment. Who's better now? Who's the one with the cool tricks?" she asked, in quite the petulant tone, shaking Natalie.

Flesh and blood were coming back to Natalie's legs. It traveled up her skin like fire on paper. Soon her neck would be vulnerable.

I faltered. I couldn't beat Molly or her suit. I might be invincible, but Natalie wasn't. She was going to die.

"Miss me?" The Rider was back. He pushed me to the ground, holding a knee on my chest. I had no lightning left.

Natalie's skin was turning normal.

Bru'G-un leaned forward to smell me. His tentacle ripped out of his wrist again. "So soft. I wouldn't think someone who was made of lightning would look so good without it."

I reached deep inside. I had been in this position before. I had barely survived. All I had was ice then. But I never ran out. Only energy had ever left me. The same was true about my lightning. I had it.

I. Was. Invincible.

I shot upward, ripping through every particle of Bru'G-un's skin. His tentacle withered and died in the dirt. His skin shriveled and a monstrous form came out. Ugly. A gaping mouth with long, rigid, sharp teeth like a shark. Purple skin that wiggled and froze. Then he fell. Nothing left.

"You killed him!" Molly spit.

"Yeah. You too."

"Not likely. Goodbye, sis. You and your monster can see the true might of the Better Suit."

The hand that gripped Natalie became fire, and her icy head that was already weakening started to melt.

I exploded. All my electricity came at my beck and call. I ripped Natalie out of the Better Suit's hand by doing what I had before. My electricity surged through the entire suit. Flashes of information hit my head, inside my brain, like I was being connected to an online server. But I reached out for the van and moved us back. Natalie collapsed into the seat and quickly changed back to skin, leaning her head on the wheel.

"No," I said. I was shaking all over. I didn't have to look in the mirror to see that my white hair had changed again. I fell backward against the seat. I still had all my energy. But my life was ebbing away.

"Go. Drive. Back to the hideout. As fast as you can. I stalled her suit, but she'll recover. We failed."

Natalie started the van and drove as fast as she could.

I sat against the back of my seat, quivering and shaking. I could still rip apart ten more Riders. I could kill anyone. But I was dying. Every burst took me out with it.

"Laoni, status," Natalie said.

"You first," I said dully.

"We're big failures. The Better Suit is too powerful for us to defeat. I was wrong. Once again, my bitch sister won."

"But we're going home," I said. "I can see Mond again."

I couldn't sleep. I couldn't faint. I just really, really wanted to!

CHAPTER 28

REDMOND

I'm here again. That sounds stupid. Anyway, I followed the trail. Almost non-existent. But it was there. More than I could even imagine. Oni, I'm on my own! Doing my own thing!

I'm having an adventure like you've had so many times when you were younger. Now I know what it's like to face danger by your lonesome. You are brave. Beautiful. Sweet. Oops, I'm not writing a love poem to you or anything. I don't have that ability.

I just want you by my side so much!

You know, I've never really thought about how easy it is to get carried away writing in this thing, telling your true thoughts to something. Okay, I am censoring a bit. I do want you to read this thing someday. And if you had even half a thought about how I imagined you here with me, you'd probably slap me hard in the face.

Yeah, it's a bit dirty. And almost physically impossible. So, I'll focus on the clean thoughts.

I've decided to be an optimist. Why? Oh, you know, because life. It's a mysterious thing.

Here we go. I followed the trail of a receipt. A simple receipt. It was caught up in all the things left behind. I didn't recognize the name. It's a small business. Lenny's Wires and Stuff.

It felt like I was chasing a ghost's tail. Why would a receipt for some electronics mean anything? And why would the owner even still be there? And how would he even know who I was talking about?

But since you are gone, and I was...imagining you dead...I'll be honest. I went anyway. It's a little store run out of a person's house far back in a forested place. How anyone could know the business was there was beyond me.

I didn't drive. Cars can be traced. I don't really want to be found. Besides, every time I steal a car, I remember how against it you were. How much you talked about the owner and how they couldn't get to work and would get fired...You rubbed off on me, Oni. I couldn't help thinking about it.

So, I am awesome, just wanted to remind you how much. I've figured out a way to move really fast without a car. I call it feet explosions. I send an explosion through my sneakers, and it propels me off the ground.

It took a few falls and bruises, but I was moving fast. I stayed out of sight and found the address on the receipt.

You'll never believe what I found!

Lenny himself. Still alive. And he had a lot of interesting stories to tell. After hours, and I mean HOURS, of him talking about the moon landing and how much he missed his chance at being an astronaut, he finally shut up to let me ask about Te'rGar.

Now, just all this wouldn't make me an optimist. You know me, Oni. I have a tendency to look on the dark side. But it was a start. What really made me think we might just win this thing after all...

Wait. A Breather is on my tail. I swear, he won't give up.

'm back. Say yay, Oni, because I evaded a Breather. Again. Oh, yes, by the way, another Breather has my scent. Couldn't help it. The bastard jumped under my feet as I tried to run away and breathed in my fire. He was fast.

But I'm running again. I have good reason. And a friend.

His name is Rust Smythe. The name itself must clue you in on that he's not exactly what you'd expect. Yeah, I forgot to tell you what I found at Lenny's. Just a minute, again!

My new companion is a bit aggravating. He asks questions all the time. He doesn't understand, even after all this time among Earthers, that there's a social etiquette to leave someone alone when writing!

Yep. Earthers. He's not of Earth.

Just wait.

～

kay, I slapped him around for bothering me. Now, let me see if I can put this in some kind of order. Lenny remembered Te'rGar. He would be in every week, asking him to get impossible things that weren't available to the general public.

Then Lenny talked for hours more about how fast of friends they became, and how he and Te'rGar, known to him as Bill Smythe, would go out bowling and talk about space and such. The two of them loved Star Trek. You haven't been bored until you listen to Lenny talk about how the Star Trek show had intricate messages the producers wanted people to know.

I showed the patience of a saint. I only burned his left eyebrow. If you knew how boring he was, you'd see that I held myself back!

Finally, he said that Te'rGar, uh, Bill, stopped coming around until he showed up with his wife and kid, begging Lenny for a different favor. Paperwork. Falsified. Then Bill left, and his wife and kid stayed behind.

Lenny helped her find a job, find a home. Then he went on and on about how strange she was and how unworldly, until he lost his other eyebrow. Finally, he, after glaring at me (who knows why—I think he hates me now), told me her address.

On my way, I met up with the Breather on my trail. I fought a few times, melted trash cans, wrapped them around the idiot who keeps coming. I think his name is Paul or something.

When I went to this person's house, I met Rust. He's about Natalie's age now. He told me how his mother, Val'Vet died of some kind of Earth sickness. I told him everything.

I didn't think it was necessary to keep it a secret.

Then, of course, the house blew up. I protected Rust, and we ran.

Then, I knew. I was with an alien. How did I know? It's logic, Oni! Breathers can't hurt humans. But as soon as I was inside, Paul attacked both of us.

When I asked Rust, he told me everything. His father was Te'r-Gar. They had come together as a family to Earth to prevent the invasion.

Invasion. You know what the invasion was? Riders. Yes! It gets cooler and more insane. I am just buzzed about how this all worked out. Turns out Te'rGar and his wife had run experiments together, repeatedly putting themselves in the machines they made, splicing their DNA. When they got word their hideout was compromised, Te'rGar agreed to draw the attack into the sky.

But he had a wife and son he wanted to protect, so he sent them away to live the best way they could, away from the war.

He died in the atmosphere. That's how Rust described it. And his mother did too. When she was sick enough, she begged to die as close to her husband as possible. So, they found a ship, got her up in the sky, and she died there like her husband had.

Why does any of this matter?

I'll give you a hint. The wife died right before the first Burner showed up.

Okay, I admit that alone is silly. Just a coincidence. If it weren't for the fact that Rust has all his parent's notes. They had a grandiose plan. They weren't just messing with DNA in order to make themselves stronger. They wanted to give Earthers the ability to fight the Riders using the only thing they had over them—the elements. At their core, no Rider can fight back against Earth's natural things.

So, their plan was to release their abilities into the atmosphere. Are you getting it? Like a bomb, both of them exploded, and when their essences went into the atmosphere, it settled down later into people and made them Burners. Or be able to bear Burners. Or whatever.

We're here because of Te'rGar. Our enemies are the Riders because that's the way it should be. A war started before either of us was even born.

Oh man! This guy is annoying. Rust is reading over my shoulder, pointing out that it's only going to get worse. I'll write as he speaks. Here we go.

"No, don't write what I'm saying. Hey, kid, are you writing what I'm saying? Fine! Okay, the Riders were stymied in the war in the sky. But they stayed. They found an ally on Earth. They're slowly but surely infiltrating everywhere. Come on, stop writing down what I'm saying. Okay, okay. I'll leave you alone."

Aha! I win!

So, Oni, don't you see? Natalie and Nora were some of the first Burners. All of us actually received the powers meant to defend Earth. And we still have to.

That's why I'm an optimist now. My whole life, I felt as if I was being punished for living for whatever I did that was so wrong. But now I know.

We're all warriors. We're Burners to defeat the aliens who would destroy us. Dun dun dun!

I feel good.

But...I miss you. I'm going back to our hideout with Rust. He might be able to look at his parents' research and figure out what else we can do. Because I've got a theory.

You know how Te'rGar created us? Well, I think his enemies created Breathers in a similar vein. Rust tells me he wasn't sure how many people were here or if they all escaped. And there were whispers of a traitor in the good side's group. That's how the secret hideout was exposed.

If the traitor told what Te'rGar and Val'Vet were doing here, it would make a whole lot of sense why Breathers and Burners seem to be so similar. They're immune to our powers and can track us anywhere.

I always wondered about that thing you told me. How Breathers after enough Burners brought in can infiltrate neighborhoods and live normally. But why? They're a good force to bring in Burners. Why let them go? Unless the ones in charge are making a secret army that can rise up at a moment's notice.

That makes sense. Way more sense than a Breather being let go when they've shown how good they are.

For many years, they've been building up. I don't even know how many Burners are left. But the bad side has been busy making an army.

Okay, I just read my last words. This is not good! How am I thinking positive? You're dying. The world's invaded and about to be ruined. Burners have mostly died out. You're dying. Rust is really annoying me, and he doesn't seem to know much about scientific stuff. You're dying! Or dead.

What is on our side? Burners, who are basically horrible in a fight. A good alien, but who knows how many there are of him?

And against us? A secret army. A secret leader named Scepter. Lots of Breathers who are just six shades of sinister. Machines that either drain us or kill us.

But, yeah, I'm going to think positively. Because the beginning of this all is that you're dying. And who the hell cares about anything else? Let the world burn if you're not in it.

So, I'm thinking. Maybe Rust could give us a cure for your condition. He has a vast amount of knowledge. And...

The best stuff. He said there might be a cure for the machines.

He doesn't know yet. He'd have to examine you. So, Oni, get your butt home and let me kiss you. Then we'll see who's dying.

Because it won't be you!

Signing off again.

I'll see you at the hideout with a whole lot to tell you.

Oh, by the way, I love you. Couldn't you figure that out? Anyway...

Bye.

CHAPTER 29

Okay, I was not in a good mood at all. I expected to go back, to lick my wounds next to Redmond. To curl up next to his side and hear that everything would be okay even if I did just run from my villain.

But Erin told me as soon as we entered that Redmond had disappeared. Where? No one knew. Why? Also, no clue.

"All I can guess is that your absence propelled him to do strange and unusual things without consulting any of us," Erin said. She too didn't look happy. Well, of course! Someone went AWOL on her watch.

She had told us both what they had found. But what did it matter? So, we have a hidden area in our secret base. Big deal!

Natalie was injured, I had run away with my tail between my legs, and this Better Suit was basically unde-featable. Oh, and the most important person in my life was gone.

"Let me see this room," Natalie said. Erin and I exchanged a look and forced her back to bed. She had worn herself out and almost died.

Cindy was bubbles and song, saying everything would be good. Everything was great. Nothing would go wrong.

Bobby and the others trusted all of us.

I wanted to be by myself.

I couldn't believe Redmond had left! Why didn't he wait for me to come back?

I checked his room for a clue. But he had only taken my diary with him. I had to believe that meant he was going to return. He wasn't heading off on some suicide mission like I had just gone on.

"Find anything?" Erin asked. She wore a mask these days, but I saw underneath it. She missed her parents, her siblings, and now she felt responsible for losing Redmond.

"Only that he took my diary, the latest one, with him. He left the rest."

Erin sat on Redmond's bed. "So, are you going to tell me what happened? I thought you were gone. I hoped…Well, let's just say it's good that you aren't dead."

"Oh, I'm all warm and fuzzy inside," I countered. I quickly explained about Natalie's sister and her suit that basically stopped any powers but had ours. Well, Erin's and Cindy's. Not mine.

"So, that's what the secret super project was." Erin held her fingers to her temples. "Natalie doesn't look good."

"She transformed into complete ice."

Erin's jaw dropped. Not much surprised her. That did. "You have gotta be kidding me. That's possible?"

"So it seems." I looked around more of Redmond's room. In the short time he had been here, he had made it his. He'd put up a few posters of his favorite sports team, whatever it was called. A few of his shirts were strewn around and he had a playlist ready to play on his stolen music player. And a small mountain of ash was on his bed. It just served to remind me of his absence.

"Why'd he leave?" I asked.

Erin threw her hands up in the air. "Because he's a jerk who I'm going to kick *so* hard he'll feel his teeth in his toes."

I shot a glare at her.

"Seriously, Laoni. The dude isn't much into this team thing. You saw him. When you left, he was always off on his own, burning junk. He found a secret room by going mad. He has anger issues. You being gone just set him off."

My ears perked up. "Are you saying finding that room made him go?"

"I guess. I wouldn't know. He left without telling me. He also took the diary of the guy. So, we're lost."

It hit me in that moment. Redmond really was off on his own mission. He had found something, something that would help. I knew him so well. There were only two reasons he'd disappear. One was because he was going to… end his own life. He was going to do that when I'd met him. But he'd tell someone. He'd say goodbye. He certainly would wait to find out for sure my status before he did. Otherwise, he'd know I'd figure out a way to bring him back to life just to slap him for it.

So, there was only one reason left. He was doing something. But Erin was right about Redmond's hatred of being in a team. He'd never tell the others what he was up to.

"Laoni, what are we going to do? We can't stay here for the rest of our lives. That diary we found, it said this place was known to the bad guys. Probably forgotten over time, but it would make sense for them to search and destroy every place we could be hiding. Especially since…" She trailed off. Her brown eyes were vacant.

"Since we failed. I failed." I sat down next to her. "You didn't think it was possible, did you?"

Erin played with her fingers. "No. When you came back right before we all died, you were this amazing hero. I thought you couldn't be defeated. This Better Suit, worn by just a normal person. She is normal, right? She doesn't have Natalie or Nora's skills…"

I thought back. No. She had technology, not powers. I quickly shook my head. "Normal. I was taken down by just a human."

Silence filled Redmond's room. His scent was everywhere, and I closed my eyes, letting his essence wash over me.

"What are we going to do?"

My eyes flashed open. "Nothing. *I'm* going to do something. I had a hostage situation. I had wasted my energy. But I'm going to just let it all build up again. Erin, secret?"

She turned toward me. Vulnerability shined in her eyes, though her face was as static as ever.

"I'm getting stronger. I can't be touched. Not when I'm full. If I was at the top, I could take her down. Boom, boom, she falls, and then…"

"So do you," Erin said. She had figured it out.

"Yeah. I'm dying. The machine took its toll. My ice is gone. I have pure energy rushing through my skin. My hair…" I pointed to the section that was dark. It was only growing wider. "I figure it's a measure of my health. When I lose all my white hair, I'm dead. One more surge, a super surge, and I go. But so does Molly, the leader of this whole thing. It was all her fault. She's the maker of the machines, the breeder of Breathers. Once she's gone, we win."

Erin punched her leg hard enough to make a sound in the room. "I thought all the sneaking around you were doing had something to do with death." She paced, kicking one of Redmond's shirts out of her way. "What about the Riders? We need to take down the Breathers' breeding grounds. Right? Or are we supposed to sit and wait while you get powered up? Because let me tell you, this is as bad as growing up in the facility knowing that every day we got closer to death. I gotta do *something*, Laoni."

I closed my eyes and I saw the information again. The stuff I had received like a message when I sparked through Molly's suit. Was it any good? It told me so much. But... could I trust it?

It took me ten seconds to realize I had no choice.

"There is a place where Riders are born. Though it's different than what we've seen. Erin, we're it, you know? Natalie is out of commission. And I won't have someone who's injured going into battle. Besides, I think she'd be against my plan."

Erin shook her head. I had to admit I had gone so fast it might have given her whiplash. "What plan?"

"I'm going to end my life. It'll end anyway soon. I'd rather go out fighting than waiting for me to waste away. The thing is, I need to get Molly so angry she'll come and take me on. Right now, she knows about my abilities."

Erin put two hands up and continued pacing the room, knocking Mond's blue shirt off his makeshift dresser. She had it in for his clothing, a representation of the guy she really wanted to punch. "This is...insane. That's what it is. Give me a second to process."

"Process what?" I demanded, standing up. "I'm dying. It's been happening since I was pushed into that machine. I don't mind. It helped us all escape."

"No!" Erin said. "You two leave. You come back and confirm that you're going to die to end this. Now you know, like, everything? What gives? Why are you so good but still going to die?"

I felt tears behind my eyes, but I'd be damned if I let Erin see. Even if they probably wouldn't even fall in the first place. "It's my powers. I *connected* with her suit. It has all the information, programmed by its mistress, and yet it betrayed her. I was online with her. She downloaded info into my head. And that's not good. It's just lucky. So, yeah, I'm going to die because I'm bad at what I do. Very bad!"

Erin scoffed. She couldn't say what she wanted to. How could she deny it? I let her parents die. I had failed at everything that was needed of me. "So, what's your plan?"

"Molly won't take me on directly. She knows what I can do. She'd avoid any fights with me. She'd take me on only at her choice. I have to make her so mad she won't see reason."

Erin picked up a pillow on Mond's bed and sent it to a fiery death. And she said Mond had a temper problem!

"And you know that so well?" Erin asked.

"I could see it in her eyes. She lets emotions run her heart. It's in her history. She started all of this because she was jealous of her sisters. I can work with that. Trust me."

"Always," Erin said.

I exhaled as I realized she meant it. "We attack the Riders and kill them all, then we get her attention. She'll come to play. I'll be ready."

Erin shook her head. "Then we'll go back to the island? By ourselves? Or…"

I gave her a pained smile. "No. You go get your family and live normally. You'll be able to. Nora and Natalie will be able to. That was always my plan. I owe it to you. Remember when we were young?"

Erin looked away. I had always told her she was being stupid. She knew before any of us that we were doomed. It was her cynicism that saved me.

"Belinda wanted all of us to escape. Not just me. I ran by myself. I didn't get the rest of you. And I've paid for that mistake all my life. I only tried to rectify it by coming back. But even that wasn't my idea. I am a coward." If only I could cry! I couldn't get this ball out of my throat!

Erin scoffed again. "No. You idiot. You aren't. You're a

pain. Better than me. And Cindy thinks the world of you. You're no coward."

I gave a shaky smile.

"I agree," a new voice added to our conversation. The most welcome voice I could have hoped for.

"Mond!" I yelled and pushed off the bed to jump into his arms. I gave him six quick kisses and then the same number of blows to his shoulder. "You idiot! Where were you?"

"Hey, Oni, come on. Don't make me look bad in front of company!"

I looked away from his way too attractive face and wonderful hair to see another guy. He was older than any of us, maybe as old as Natalie.

He had a shock of red hair that reached his chin. He was ruggedly good-looking with velvety smooth brown eyes. There was something otherworldly to him. A shine to his eyes. Longer chin. Too many freckles going down his neck. Don't get me wrong, he looked like he was from Earth. But something in me told me he wasn't.

"Laoni, meet Rust Smythe. He's an alien. He's going to save you."

Erin's eyes widened. I wished I could feel any hope.

But my fate was sealed.

CHAPTER 30

Rust had explored the entire area before he told me how exactly he convinced Mond he was going to save me. He was busy reliving childhood memories. Rust had spent four years of his childhood in this place.

He moved from room to room, making little a-ha noises and then went back to the secret area.

The secret area was actually a lot bigger than I'd imagined. Made of concrete like every other room, it stretched out far into the back with lots and lots of empty space. I could tell different kinds of machinery used to be in there, but all that was left was one little area of filing cabinets. One gaping hole showed Mond's first entry into the room, and the open door right into Cindy's room, which she couldn't figure out how to close, was on the other side.

Everyone was interested in what Rust's diagnosis of me would be. It didn't take long for Erin to let the cat out of the bag that I was dying. You'd think someone really important was meeting her end, not me. But they all looked like their best friend was.

I hadn't gotten much of a chance to talk to most of my

team, and I just leaned back against the wall as I watched them watch Rust.

I had no hope in this new alien. He was already a little sketchy. He burst out with inappropriate things all the time. Like when he first came in, he automatically sized up who was in a relationship and who wasn't.

"Ah, you two," he pointed at me and Mond. "You two," he added about Cindy and Erin. "Not you two." That was Bobby and Kenya.

There were two others on our team. They had come with the second group Nora sent. Frankie, an Ice Burner, and Jeff, also Ice. I didn't really know them as I hadn't spoken to them much. Rust said nothing about them.

Instead, he was off again, going a million miles a minute. When he found out Natalie was injured, he quickly asked to be able to take a look at her, which told me he was a doctor. But he didn't say much about himself at all.

Mond filled me in. Rust was a child of two aliens who had been fighting Riders. I read his diary. I really liked reading his diary entries…Anyway, when Rust checked out Natalie, he nodded a few times and said, "Ah, no wonder. You, my dear, haven't been getting the proper nutrition. Every body works better with what it needs, even Burners."

She was *not* happy. "I eat what I eat. It's just the fact I'm burnt out."

He shook his head. Natalie glared even more. "Not true! It's a nice excuse. But the fact is that if you had eaten a proper diet before going into ice form, it wouldn't have knocked you out so badly."

Natalie hissed at him and shook off the blood pressure cuff he had asked someone to scrounge up. "I'm fine. We have more important things to do. And why does everyone have to be in here?"

I looked behind me. Bobby was taking over the doorway,

but I saw Kenya's face peeking in, and Cindy and Erin were hanging over Bobby's shoulders. Frankie and Jeff were outside but still listening to the conversation.

"Face it," I said, showing a chipper face. "You're our leader."

"No, you are," Cindy's voice echoed out over Bobby's shoulder.

I ignored her. "So, um, Rust…"

He turned to me, arching an eyebrow. "Call me Doctor."

I gaped at him. He was unbelievable. "Um, Doctor. Is she okay?"

"Nothing that a good diet and rest won't help her recover from."

Natalie sat up further. "I am a grown woman. No one tells me what to eat. Look," she added to waylay his argument, "I don't know who you are."

"Doctor Smythe: Burner expert. On the run, thanks to one of yours. Here to save her." He pointed at me.

Again, I just shook my head.

"Oh, and you can call me Rust."

Natalie looked like she wanted to call him something a little more rude.

"Speaking of which," he added, looking toward me, "this is as good as any time to check you over." He clicked his tongue to indicate that Natalie needed to get out of her bed and I should replace her.

"Get out of my room!" Natalie yelled.

We thought it was best to listen to her. Well, all except me. "Natalie, is he right?" I asked, sliding to the end of her bed. "Are you okay?"

Natalie's face tightened. "Probably. I never thought about it. But I do feel differently when I eat differently. But that's beside the point. Where did Redmond find *him*?"

"Long story." I still didn't get the luck that tied him to our fates, especially if he was what he seemed. We had no clue about how our bodies worked. Rust seemed to have in-depth knowledge. And how many injuries did we have on a regular basis? It had taken Kenya and Bobby weeks of healing, way longer than they should have, when they had been injured on the island.

If we sent him there, we could have a much-needed ally. And that was nothing compared to what Rust had said about saving me. A cure for the machine. A fix for an Alternate Burn.

"But you trust him?" she asked.

"Do you?" I countered.

She gritted her teeth. "I hate him. He's abrasive. Arrogant. Plus, he's the offspring of people who ruined my life." She was quiet. She hadn't taken it as well as Redmond when she found out how this whole thing started.

I understood. If it weren't for his parents, all of us would have been fine with our families. I'd still have Mom and Dad. Natalie and Nora might not have gotten along with Molly, but she wouldn't have started a secret organization to kill us all.

"We wouldn't know each other," I added to her what-if-ing brain. "I wouldn't have met Mond. Or Erin, Cindy, or even…Belinda."

Natalie reached out and squeezed my hand. She knew how much Belinda meant to me. "It would have been a different life."

"But not better," I whispered.

"You're dying!" Natalie said. "How is that not the worst thing?"

I gave her a small smile. "Because I have gotten so much joy out of this life. The relationships. The friends. But, also, my ice was so beautiful. I put a piece of myself in every sculpture. I wouldn't have wanted to lose that even if I only had it for a little while." I looked into Natalie's eyes. "I choose this life. Wouldn't you?"

Natalie didn't answer. She didn't like telling me I was right. She wanted to hate Rust. And right now, that was fine with me.

"Chop chop, dying light! Let's go. Rage and rage some more," Rust said, sticking his head in the room. "If this room won't work, then I'll set up an examination room in the secret but not so secret any more room. Oh, and *you* should be resting and eating kale!" That was directed at Natalie.

Natalie threw her pillow at him, but his head zipped out before it hit him.

"I really despise him," she noted.

I held back a giggle. Rust was annoying. But…I don't know why. He was growing on me, like a rash.

I dutifully followed him to the secret room. He had given orders to fill it with tables, like a little hospital. I wondered how much he thought we'd need it. Mond followed me in.

Rust held up his hand as I settled down on the table. "Nuh-uh. You can't be here unless Laoni wants you here. Do you want him here?"

I considered. Though I wouldn't mind him holding my hand, I didn't want him to know for sure what the final prognosis would be. Maybe I could keep it secret. Natalie wasn't the only one who would object to my ultimate plan— my final plan.

"Go, Mond. I'll see you later."

He looked back. hurt, but he understood. He glanced at Rust. "Hey, take care of her. And don't ask her annoying questions."

Rust gave him a look. "I *never* ask annoying questions. I ask good questions. But you are gone now, so go!"

Mond took one final glance at me and scooted out the burnt-out exit.

"How long?" Rust asked as he started looking into my eyes, lifting my hair and letting it fall again, then scribbling some notes down.

"How long what?"

"Choose. How long were you in the machine and how long has it been since you were?"

I closed my eyes and thought back. Pain. All that pain. Almost giving up. Then all the deaths. "Forever. A few minutes. I don't know. Oh, and it's been about a year, I think. I don't keep a record of time much."

"Your diary?"

I glared at him. "I don't keep dates."

He nodded. "Okay." He held up one arm to his face. Weird stuff happened. Veins the color of molten lava roared under his skin. Scanning me?

He asked me a lot of questions, not just annoying ones. Personal ones. I let it all hang out. I wasn't going to get anywhere by hiding anything.

At the end of my examination, he sighed and jumped up on an opposite table, swinging his legs. "You're being used up by your power."

I wanted to slap him. Or punch him. Or just knee him really hard in the gut. "No duh."

He didn't care. "Every time you use it, you basically pour your blood out. Soon it will be gone."

"Is there any kind of, you know, transfusion I could get?"

"No."

That was it then. Hopes gone. Redmond was wrong. Rust had been dead wrong.

"There's really nothing I can do for you. If you'd been in the machine for only a minute or if it had been a month, there might have been something. But the only answer now is…"

"Are you done yet?" Mond's voice came yelling.

I groaned. "Come in here." I guess keeping it a secret from him was out of the question.

His wonderful body appeared in the opening. "Oh, only if you want me here."

I beckoned him forth with my fingers, and he came to hold my hand. "Doctor Smythe was just about to tell me how hopeless it was, Mond. I'm sorry."

He gripped my hand. His face crumpled, but not too much. He had already accepted it. And he never had much in the way of optimism.

"There's nothing?" Mond asked.

"One thing." Rust crunched his lips up a little.

Both of us stared at him.

"Story time!" he yelled and clicked his fingers to get Redmond to sit next to me.

"I don't want a story. I just want…"

Rust cut me off. "My parents ran from my home worlds of light years away from where we are now. I've never known any other home, but they told me all about it. The Riders, what you call them, were the Imposters. They pretended to be part of our world and took over slowly but surely from within. Destroyed it. Nothing was left except a small spaceship with my people on it. But the Riders had sights on another planet. A beautiful blue and green gem that would lift them up."

"I so don't care," I said.

Rust wasn't listening. "The main Rider had technology that stripped away Burner's attributes, which made the machine. My parents stole the machines that gave stuff back. That's what was used to enhance their DNA. It gave them Earth's elements."

I still didn't get what that had to do with me.

"If this place was stripped bare," he said, "then that main Rider has the technology."

"Bru'G-un? He's dead now."

Rust stopped and smiled. "Then you have my thanks. You gave me vengeance. But where is his machinery? He stole it all from here, from my parents."

I realized in a second who had the machines. "Molly has them."

"Then that's your answer. Get the opposite machine, and it should bypass what happened to you. Stay in as long as you can. A day. A month. A year. Whatever. Then you'll be back to your own."

I imagined it. Having my ice again. Making my art. Being whole. "Would it be in the Rider's breeding ground?" I asked.

Rust held up his finger. "No. This stuff is powerful. It's a tool to make Burners, kind of. My parents figured it out. But they had to die to give the powers to people. The point is, there is no way your—Molly, did you say?—would let it out of her sight. She knows where it is. And only she will be able to lead you to it."

Rust silenced and stood up. He gave me a comforting squeeze on my arm. "Sorry for the grim news. If only I had been here earlier. If only I had known the extent they were going to. I had no idea there was so much stuff under my nose."

"Yeah, where were you?" Mond asked. He sounded angry.

"Fighting an endless fight with something you wouldn't believe." He looked away. He was serious. But I didn't care. Let everything go. We had a job to do. Even if I could find Molly before we attacked her next place, she wouldn't tell me. There was no way. It was just as hopeless as everything else.

"Come on, Mond. We have some resting to do. We need to take out another breeding hole soon." I pulled on his arm and we walked off.

I heard Rust mutter under his breath. "I'm so sorry."

I didn't like Rust any more than I had before. I had a little burning hope deep inside that he was going to help me. Mond had the same feeling. But it had crashed us down again. I saw nothing but my end.

"Stay with me tonight," I told Mond.

He held me, murmuring sweet promises in my ear. Little did he know how soon we'd have to say goodbye. I hadn't changed my plan.

I would still kill Molly and destroy that Better Suit. It made it even worse now that she had information that could save me. I couldn't be distracted by that.

"Maybe you should rethink things," Mond whispered, stroking my arm. "I mean, if you pushed her into it, you have this ultimate power. Her death or the cure…"

I shook my head, bumping into his chest. "You didn't see that suit. It changes everything. Natalie couldn't fight it. None of us can. She can wipe Burners out. She can fly and find our hideout. I can't risk her getting away just for my life. I *can't*."

Mond wrapped his arms around me. I fell asleep.

Tomorrow we were going to fight again. Then we'd draw Molly out. I wouldn't even consider there was a save for me. I couldn't split my efforts. For all of them. For the people I'd once betrayed and for the ones I'd allowed to be hurt.

No, I was dead. I accepted that. But I'd take Molly out with me.

CHAPTER 31

*D*iary,

    It's hard to write in you now. So much has been happening, and now knowing that I'll probably let Mond read this changes how I think and how I write it down. I suppose I could go back to letting it be only my own thoughts, my secret, but I don't know. It's freeing knowing I'm telling Mond all my thoughts.

    I'll continue to be honest. Hi, Mond! I hope you can read these words and be comforted far into the future when I'm gone and all that is left is my memory.

    So, what's been happening? Well, after Smythe gave me the devastating news, we went back to normal. Everyone here is so maudlin. Like, "Poor Laoni, she's going to die." I hate it. I'm upset. Blah, blah, blah.

    I've accepted it. Why can't they?

    Now that everyone knows I'm dying, I almost told them all my plans. I told Mond. He doesn't agree, but I think he understands. Do you, Mond? Do you see why I'd rather go out making a safer place for Burners than just waiting for my energy to run out?

    On the bright side, Natalie is doing better. The plan for the raid on the Riders happens tomorrow. We've spent a week preparing. No one questioned how I knew the location. I think it's silly. I certainly would question the knowledge, but I am their hero. I can do no wrong.

Rust is settling in here. There's plenty of room. He took Cindy's room. She didn't want to be next to the hidden passageway while Rust did, thanks to his parents and feeling closer to them.

He hasn't told us everything about himself. I don't not trust him, but I can't trust him either. He won't tell us where he's been all this time or if he knew so much about Burners why he was nowhere to be found as many were gathered up and executed.

Rust really is annoying. He's also right, which makes it worse. He pointed out again how loud a Volkswagen bus was and how we couldn't exactly drive it into a quiet neighborhood without drawing suspicion. He also told us how much he didn't like being trapped in a tin can when he's traveling, so Natalie sent out Mond and Bobby to steal a giant SUV. We'll all fit, which is good because we're all going. Natalie has told Nora and said her goodbyes.

Oh, yeah, Natalie's coming with us. She said, "Yeah, I'm fine. You know what I can do. And I've been eating my kale." She thinks Smythe is right.

But he's aggravating and really rubbing Natalie the wrong way. She feels like she leads, no question. She gives orders and everyone listens. Not Rust. He questions everything. He follows her, of course. But he sure raises many thoughts that we didn't think of before.

For example? The Rider raid. He asked what our morals were. Whether we knew we'd be killing babies and if that bothered us.

It didn't before. I thought of them as evil. But I know what those babies grow into. It can't stop my resolve, not when those babies would turn into the monsters that helped kill a whole lot of Burners.

Of course, I say that now. But if we go into the building and there are a bunch of helpless squalling babies, I don't know what I'll do.

I'll burn that bridge when we come to it, I guess. I made a choice. This is a war. And the small number of Riders I've met were more evil than the Breathers. In fact, it seemed that their evil permeated the Breathers, minus Drake for some unknown reason.

Their goal is to torture and kill. That's it. They're practically invulnerable, and only our elements hurt them. That kind of power can't be allowed to continue, especially if Rust is right and they're still planning on invading.

Oh, yes, another gem from our good doctor. He tells us that there was no way they gave up, even if they were stymied. And all the Breathers succeeding and infiltrating human areas? Part of a long-term attack plan.

Rust is a font of information. His parents left him with their notes and a mission. Riders can't procreate easily. There is only one female born to every sixty men. That female is kept safe and secreted away, meant for only creating a child.

So, when we attack their breeding ground, we're not going to come across monstrous gelatinous goo. It will be a mother. Will I falter?

Not sure. Can't tell. I feel numb. Like every day that I get closer to death, I become less...me.

Yes, Mond, I still love you. Oh, did I have to tell you that too? But every other feeling has morphed into conviction. I will not fail. I will rid this world of a threat to me and my kind.

It's getting close to time. I still can't sleep. I'm abuzz with light. Even with total darkness, I can see easily. Anyone could.

Mond is curled up next to me. He won't leave my side. I keep a blanket between us. I'll hurt him if I don't. I don't want to hurt him. I don't want to hurt anyone ever again.

That's why I have to kill the Riders.

Gotta go. I have to shake Mond awake and go over our plan of *action once more. After breakfast, and a lot of discussion, we'll meet everyone out by the SUV.*

It's time to destroy the last Breathers—the Riders.

It's time to see how strong I really am.

Scepter kept secrets really well, hidden underground or in forests. They knew how to avoid detection. This one took the cake, though. If I ever wondered where all the Riders came from before they infiltrated the neighborhoods they lived in, I shouldn't have.

Hovering over the neighborhood was their mothership. It was invisible, of course.

Rust told us that we could expect the entrance to be seen and then blend into the invisible part so when they exited it, it wouldn't look like they came from nowhere.

So, the camouflaged front door was to a little yellow mobile home. It looked like a tiny wooden porch, swollen from rain and sagging in certain parts.

We all looked at Rust like he was crazy. If it weren't for the address that had come into my head when I connected with Molly's suit, I would think I was the insane one.

"Trust me, don't be deceived by appearances. The Riders *love* hanging out in less than obvious places."

We had arrived in our black SUV with tinted windows. Redmond and Bobby were good at stealing now. The hideout was somewhat out in the sticks in a dirty, dusty mobile home park with lots of space between the homes. This one had an acre around it. As I looked up into the sky, I could see almost like a heat rainbow wriggling.

"I guess we should go," I said. "Natalie?"

Natalie shifted. Everyone gasped when she became perfect ice.

She laughed. "Don't think this is amazing. Wait until we're done with this. Look, keep it together, people. If we win, this is about it. The forces will have no more recourses. All we'll have to worry about is the leader and the ones already in place. But we can deal with that. Keep together. Go in tight. Use whatever elements you can use."

"And stay behind me," I added. Everyone agreed.

Rust was armed as well. He was coming in, too. He had a weapon of his own, not like Drake's. Rust's was a flame thrower. We had been really busy preparing for this.

"I'll stick with Rust," Erin said. She liked to have fire at her fingertips, stuff she could actually throw at the bad guy without worries. I wondered if any of them knew how hard it was to take down a Rider. Or if any of them would falter if they saw helpless babies.

Inside I begged, *Let them be grotesque!*

But it was time. It was past time.

We roared down the street and jumped out as soon as we got in front of the mobile home. It was the middle of the day. No one was around. Everyone was at work or far enough away not to notice our commando team.

I felt a bit ridiculous, like I was in one of those movies where suits poured out of a black car and surrounded a building. It got worse as we stomped up the rickety stairs and kicked down a really weak door.

Then, once we got inside, everything was proven not so insane.

There was a completely silver ramp. The guards were Breathers.

We fought a skirmish.

It was no contest. I was blazing light, knocking them down. It felt so good to not worry about them getting my scent as I crumpled them in front of me and ran up the ramp.

It opened to a huge hangar-like area with a gigantic open door on the other side. The interior was open machinery, lots of whirring gears like Molly's suit. The floor was a metallic silver that echoed our footsteps.

Alarms blared. Red flashed everywhere.

Breathers poured in, intent on taking us down. There were a lot more guards here than anywhere else.

Across the way, Rust poured flames onto our makeshift battleground while Erin designated where they went. Redmond melted the metal under him and used his fire to force it around his attackers, making silver burritos.

Cindy froze the floor, and our attackers became frozen— convenient targets. Jeff and Frankie followed suit. Bobby just climbed as high as he could and melted the roof and any other metal he could find, which would fall down like molten rain, catching the Breathers in their hair and setting that on fire too.

But they kept coming.

I blazed a path through, heading toward the door.

Inside, it was like an apartment building, all square and boxlike. I was like a lightning storm. Nothing could touch me. I zapped and zipped, trying to figure out where the nursery was. Hoping I wouldn't have to go from door to door, killing anyone inside.

Why did I feel very much like the bad guy?

That feeling changed lightning-quick.

A Rider came running out of one of the doorways. A female Rider. You know how I could tell?

She didn't look human. The monstrous thing I had seen when Bru'G-un died was in all her glory. Big round lips with a stinger protruding from them. Tall as a stop sign. Six pincher-like arms.

"Get inside!" a voice yelled. Ah, a Rider. A male one. The female turned around and slipped back inside, spilling acid as she walked.

Gross.

"You will not stop our future!" he yelled at me. "Die!"

He spun toward me, bringing his hands together in an overhead strike. He crumpled before he touched me.

"Not too bright," I taunted. I looked around again. There was one big room at the end. A force field was in place there. Red flashed everywhere.

I ran toward the force field and walked right through. It sizzled and went out and I opened the door. Babies…

I guess they were, anyway. The whole area had squares of boxes with lumps in them. They were little balls of goop, much purpler than I expected. The only thing developed on them were big gaping mouths. And here's the most disgusting thing I could think of. Half of the balls of goop were in…what looked like the skin of babies. Real babies. Human babies. And as they grew, they melded with this skin.

Where the Riders had gotten the skin or… Never mind. Couldn't go there. It just reinstated my horror about these things. They were an invasion. An imposter, just like Rust said.

I burst. I threw everything in me into taking all of them out. I didn't stop as the balls of goop burst. I kept exploding. I was making sure.

But I was also testing. How much could I explode? When I took down Molly, I'd need more power.

Suddenly, a blue alarm added to the red. A strange language filled the air. With the rumbling, I could guess what was happening. I had brought down the place from the inside.

All hands abandon ship. Those who could still walk anyway.

Mission accomplished.

I rushed out of the room, slipping as the ship started turning on its side. Redmond came running around the corner, falling.

"Laoni!"

"Out that way!" I yelled. "We're going down. Get out. Now!"

He didn't listen. He came toward me and grabbed me into a hug. I didn't know how bad I looked. Who cared?

We were done. There'd be no new Riders, Runners, or Bloodhounds.

Burners were safe.

After we escaped the ship that was.

REDMOND

*H*iya Laoni,

I know, you'd say I should get my own diary now. But I don't know. I feel closer to you writing in this. I'm going to keep this entry a secret, though. I'm hiding it between the pages you already wrote, somewhere between descriptions of Breathers and an account of your history. Maybe you'll find it someday. But I don't mind as long as we have a someday. I'm pouring it all out there, and I don't want you seeing what my plan is.

We liberated the Burners by attacking a hidden ship filled with Riders. I saw you in battle, and I almost got myself killed. You were that amazingly beautiful. I couldn't believe that you, my girl right there, had deigned to talk to me, to be with me. We're united.

I couldn't believe how lucky I was. Then, when we left that crashing ship as fast as our car could go, I watched your hair turn almost completely black. One strip of white was left. One more burst, and you're dead.

And that's your plan.

I realized something. I am in love with you in every way. My soul is connected to yours. My destiny is entwined with yours. If you say you must die, then I will too. That's it.

But it would be a crime greater than anything I could think of for a light like you to go out. That's what you are—a light in the darkness. When I was alone, I lived like an animal. I always wondered what it'd be like to rejoin humanity. Every single time, I realized I would be a great menace to them. I'd kill anyone I'd touch.

But not you. When you found me— You might say that I found you, but no. You discovered me. Found me. Took me out of my darkness and illuminated my world. When that happened, I was alive again.

The journeys we've had, the adventures, the people we've met. You were always you, fighting alongside me. Nothing was impossible, even finding a fairy tale island. It was real. You made it real.

If you wonder why I'm going overboard telling you how much you mean to me, I just had to let you know that I won't let you die.

I can't.

I'm devising a plan. I'm not waiting for this command. I'm going to do it. It's dangerous. Maybe I'm putting us all in danger. But I don't really care. You've saved so many. We can handle the danger.

Because, Oni, I will live a half-life if you are gone. I won't have my light go out.

It was an amazing time. You know, after we defeated the last of the Breathers' hideouts. I know there are still facilities out there where Burners are kept, but Natalie thinks we can easily find them now. The war has turned.

Do you want to know when I got my idea? When you told me about Natalie and what she did when you found the Better Suit. I won't give spoilers here. You still might find this. Let's just say, when you wonder where I am these days, I'll tell you here. I'm way out under the dam, as far back as I can go, practicing my flames. I will move on to the next level. I've spent a whole lot of time with Natalie, learning what it's like to grow up with powers and what she had to do to get her skills.

I'm going to save you, Oni. We will live. You won't have that one last burst.

That's it. Like I said, I don't want to spoil anything here. More than anything, I don't want you stopping me. Of all the people here, I know you could.

I hear you looking for me. I'm hiding this now. I'll put the diary back and you won't know it was gone.

Bye, but only for today. Not forever. There won't be a forever! You are going to live.

CHAPTER 34

It was almost like we were back on the island. We were going to head there in a week or so, but Natalie wanted to make sure all the facilities were gone. That wasn't my plan at all. Natalie may have thought she knew her sister, but she didn't. Not really.

Natalie thought Molly would just disappear, having been routed so utterly. I wasn't so sure. In fact, I was betting on Molly coming after us. I laid a trap. I sent a message through one of the Breathers that wouldn't leave us alone. Paul is getting to be a real annoyance. All he can do is mainly make faces at us and run. That's what he's good at.

But I asked him to deliver a message to her. If she wanted to go one-on-one with me again, meet me at an old stadium. Blah, blah, blah. As I expected, she sent a message back to me as quickly as she could, saying, "Bring it on."

I had a feeling the defeat of her possible future invasion would anger her enough to take me up on my challenge.

For everyone else, this was peacetime. They were going out and actually seeing movies, having frozen yogurt, and enjoying the summer.

For me, it wasn't so simple. It never was. I was going to go out and leave them a future. If only Mond would have agreed with me. I think he was angry. I checked my diary for new entries, but he had stopped writing. Maybe he had done as I suggested and gotten his own, but he wasn't anywhere near me.

He was always gone. I'd see him for meals, but the rest of the time, he was missing.

The preparations for going home were nearing completion. The last facilities would be liberated, and then we'd all go home.

They would, I should say.

Natalie suggested that I stay out of the future liberations, and I agreed, surprising her. Little did she know that I was going to be part of a different liberation—to keep the future safe for everyone.

I didn't bother doing anything to prepare for my battle with Molly. I just put a nice outfit on. My best defense. It would shock Molly, I hoped, to have a Burner appear in a ballgown. It was very elegant. Unfortunately, it wasn't made of the same crazy material that helped me regulate my powers, so as long as I wore it, I couldn't eat or drink anything. My electricity was worse than ice. It really destroyed everything that came in.

The dress was gorgeous, though, something I'd always imagined wearing. It was long and silver with lots of gold beads, making flowery rain down to the skirt at my ankles. The sleeves were like red daggers pointing to my wrists. I had found it in a thrift store and actually paid for it…with money I stole from an ATM. I'm not proud.

When the rest of my friends got ready to go take down a facility—Mond was still nowhere to be found, but I guess he went with them—I prepared. I wished I was getting ready for a dance with Redmond on my arm and not a battle, but I wasn't. I pinned my hair up into a beautiful bun and placed a tiara on my head. I was lucky my skin itself didn't burn it off.

I did the whole Cinderella thing and ordered a horse-drawn coach. I made the driver raise his eyebrows. He could barely speak the whole journey. But I was on my way. I couldn't even say goodbye to Mond. I couldn't believe he had let me go. I knew he was angry, but come on!

I should have said a farewell in my diary. But I couldn't even write.

The streets slowly disappeared under the wheels and I looked down at the road, lonelier than I had ever felt. This whole to-do hadn't done much to cheer me up. I was going to my own death. I would take Molly out with me, but tell that to my heart! I didn't want to die.

I didn't want to leave Mond or my friends. I wanted to see how everything turned out. With Cindy and Erin. With Natalie. Even with Rust Smythe, who had asked to go along with Natalie to the island so he could help out.

My heart broke when I thought about Mom, who spent so many years searching for me only to find out I wouldn't ever come home. I thought about Drake and how he was the one Breather to have a conscience. I wanted to know how. And Gem! My only sister. The one who accepted me and looked up to me. I wanted to be her role model. I wanted to gently guide her through the ice symptoms, if she had them, the growing she'd need to do as she got a hold on any power. More, I wanted to see if a Breather's blood would make her more or less powerful.

I was going to lose all of that. And Mond! My fire man. My flame. My heat. I had wanted a future with him, doing all the stuff that people our age did. Growing together and seeing what happened when Burners grew old.

All gone.

The driver looked back at me again, like he had done for the umpteenth time. My sad face gave him courage.

"So, you heading to a party?" he asked. "Or running away?"

Funny, I hadn't had a lot of experience interacting with people who had no idea on how the Burners' world worked. Who were oblivious to the secret lives right under their noses. I looked at him, at his sallow cheeks and balding head. He looked like a dripping candle. But he was sincere. The sympathy in his eyes matched the complete and utter adoration he radiated.

"I'm running to my destiny."

His forehead wrinkled. He didn't get it. And I wouldn't explain it to him. He had the address. He looked more than confused when he scanned the area and saw no other cars, only an abandoned stadium.

"This the right address?" he asked, clicking to his horse.

"Yes. Thank you." I gave him the rest of my money. All I had. His eyes widened.

"Hey, you already paid. I can't leave you here."

"Yes, you can," came a voice to our left.

A Breather, Paul, looking happier than ever. He must have thought I was finally going to die. Silly fool.

The driver didn't like Paul's look. "Um, you have me for an hour," he informed me. "I can let my horse rest and then..."

Paul turned dagger eyes on him. "Leave. Now. She's well taken care of, believe you me."

The driver blanched. But I gave him a smile. "I'm perfectly okay. We're just role-playing a Cinderella-type thing. He's my Prince Charming."

The driver gave me a dubious look, but he couldn't stay. I was fine. He could tell I wanted him gone, and Paul was giving off his creepy aura. He turned his horse and I watched my Cinderella dreams drive away. I wasn't going to a ball.

Paul took me in and gasped a few times. He was ready for his reaction, though. So, he only grabbed my arm and pushed me forward.

"Well, I don't know what you planned," he said, "but Molly is already here. And she's ready to kill you."

I shook Paul's grasp off me and gave him a look. "You're a survivor, right?"

He pushed his shoulders to his ears. "Yeah."

"Then you'd better run. I'm going to kill everything here. Good luck."

He stepped back, cocked his head, and then took me seriously. Smart Breather. He turned on his heels and ran.

I walked past the overgrown parking lot to the large doors of the stadium. I saw Molly in her suit, flying from end to end, waiting for me. It was time for my destiny.

It was time to defeat my enemy once and for all.

The sheer size of the empty stadium pressed down on me. I had been in battles, had fought to save my life countless times. But to actually walk into a place that would spell out my own death? And not by my enemy's hands but by my own?

Surreal didn't cover it.

"Welcome!" Molly yelled as she saw me. She stopped flying in the air to stare at me. Her eyes were narrowed to a point, and I could see a thick vein practically jumping out of her forehead. "I really hope you're not relying on your perverted beauty to make me go nuts because I'm over that. Beauty is a lie, and I am immune!"

Great. There went that theory. I'd gotten dressed up for nothing.

Molly swooshed through the sky, flipping her braids of

blonde hair. "You have nerve, I'll give you that. Did you actually think you could win?"

The empty seats all around me echoed her words, slipping seamlessly into space. "Yes, actually, I did," I shouted back to her.

Slowly I commanded my spark to start up. I was getting good at this. If it weren't for the small and minor detail that every time I used my powers I was draining myself, I'd be unstoppable.

One thread at a time, my princess dress flipped into pure energy, and I jumped into the air.

I circled my enemy. Molly looked so much like Natalie, not as much as Nora, of course, but she had similar eyebrows, a chin that matched. But it was her eyes that were most different. Full of contempt, of hatred. Who knew that what was in the eyes could make someone ugly or beautiful? I would call Natalie beautiful. But her sister was back-of-a-donkey ugly.

"I thought you'd chicken out," Molly said casually. "But I should have known. Anyone bold enough to ruin my life so utterly would show up again!"

"This battle doesn't have to happen." I was still clinging to one last shred of hope. Something to keep me alive a little longer. Something that might make the sisters come together again. A peace treaty.

"Oh, no?" Molly sneered. She snapped her suit's gloves and six missiles launched to hover above her head.

"This enmity doesn't have to exist. You have sisters. You turned on them. But..." I was desperately trying to find another ending. My lightning skirt flowed out around me. "Can't we have peace? We've utterly destroyed your invasion."

Molly laughed out loud. "You think that, do you? You are a child. For years, we've planned this. There are Breathers all over the country. There are Riders all over the world. Three breeding grounds? Was that really all you thought there were? My sister should have told you…"

The missiles flew toward me, spinning and shining in the setting sun. Somehow, I didn't want them exploding anywhere near me. I sent a tendril of lightning at them. They exploded in huge balls of flame, shaking the stadium and me. Yep, really didn't want them near me.

"I never give up. I will eradicate you all!" Molly screamed. Twelve more missiles shot toward me. I flew and dodged them as best I could. But one connected with my energy.

Bam!

I shot across the air, slamming headfirst into a row of empty seats. I was still on my feet.

Suddenly, I was being attacked from below.

Everything hit my electricity and fizzled, but the shock waves were incredible. I shook as waves of percussion took hold of my body.

I flew, trying to get my bearings. Molly came after me.

With a fist to my cheek—the lightning took the blow and sizzled her armor—I flew again. She was very good.

I slammed into the ground, pushing the dirt into a pile around me. I saw who was shooting at me. Riders. Cannons. Guns.

With a crunch to my fist, I sent a wave of pure lightning at them all. They screamed in unison and crumpled.

I was building up. I was getting ready to explode.

I powered my way back up next to Molly and wrapped my arms around her suit. I was gratified to hear it starting to spark and fail. Red hot heat built up under me.

"Want to hug a volcano?" Molly asked. "Keep holding on, you stinking, little freak!"

My energy protected me. But the suit was doing some stuff. I let go. I had to end it. There was no more holding back. This woman had brought back up to a one-on-one battle. She had betrayed her sisters and tried to kill all the Burners. I had to go out now, like a snuffed candle.

But I was taking her with me.

First wave...blow.

Molly screamed as her suit broke into pieces and stopped working. The gears stopped. She still had waves and waves of arsenal. She was still fighting. She was still flying.

I lit up again.

Second wave, go.

I exploded again and lit up the stadium. Nothing below us was alive. Nothing was left.

Molly glared at me and spit.

Of course, it hit the inside of her face shield, so all it did was dribble down. I almost felt sorry for her.

Almost.

One last move would destroy the suit. And the missiles that were still coming out. If they hit me, I was dead anyway. It was time to go out. Goodbye...

Third wave...

Huh?

All I felt was heat. Pushing me. Hugging me. Another attack from Molly?

Flames... Had I attacked and died? Was this hell? Had I truly been judged?

But it felt so warm. So loving. Almost like a hug. And a kiss? It went along my cheek, going right through my lightning.

"No, Oni, you don't have to die. I can't let you."

It was no hell! It was Mond, my personal heaven.

My eyes focused to see a man of pure fire, like Natalie's ice. His eyes were round balls of flame in a face of molten lava. His clothing could be seen as lines, but they had become lines of fire. What I could see was almost like a prince's outfit. Long tails, flowing pants, and a nice fiery crown on his head.

"What's this?"

"You wore a Cinderella dress. It's only fitting that I'm your Prince Charming."

I shook my head. "What are you doing?" I asked.

Molly gave me the finger and then she flew off. So fast I couldn't stop her.

"Mond! She has more Riders. She has more forces. She needs to be stopped. Her suit can still be used!"

"I can't let you die. That's it." He let go of me. I let my power slip back inside.

"Oh, Mond. I was going to sacrifice myself. It's not going to happen today, but I will die. Don't you understand anything?"

Mond nodded. His wonderful blond hair came back. The flames left his eyes. His prince's outfit became blue and gold. He hugged me again and caressed my jaw. "Ow," he noted. "That still hurts." But he wouldn't let me go.

"Mond!" I cried. "Now Molly will be around when I'm dead. You have no idea how dangerous she is."

"I don't care. You will live."

I tried very hard to be angry at him, but I couldn't. "I will die."

He shook his head and helped me up. Everything was crumpled from my attacks or Molly's. The stadium wasn't even standing anymore. "The Better Suit couldn't feel when I put my flame tracer on. Come on. We've gotta hurry."

I gaped at him. He had learned that? What had he been doing?

"Stop gaping," he said with a grin. "We gotta follow her."

His feet lit up. I know what I read in my diary. He had told me what he could do. But I guess I hadn't trusted in it until he picked me up and leaped into the air, pouring flames under his feet to make him a human rocket.

I relaxed against his arm. I had no idea what was going on, but it sure felt good to be carried by him. "Mond, it's over. I don't have the machines that will save me."

"But Molly does," he insisted. "And wherever she's going now to fix her busted ass suit is where it will be. That's why I waited to stop you. You cut it pretty close. I almost couldn't save you."

I leaned my head on his shoulder, wondering what was going on, and what he hoped for. "I didn't want to be saved."

"Too bad for you. Let's go. We're not done with Molly yet."

I looked into his eyes. There was a red flame pointing toward the tracer he had presumably used on Molly.

I was having a bit of trouble accepting this turn of events. I was ready to die. I was willing. I had said my goodbyes to everyone. I wasn't even sure I wanted to live any longer. I had done so much harm in my life. I'd had so much done to me.

But I realized as Mond clutched me tightly, it didn't matter what I wanted. He couldn't live without me. Neither could my family. And it'd hurt Natalie for her to come back from the raid on the last facilities to find out I had sacrificed myself.

Somehow everything I had done seemed grotesquely wrong.

"Do you…really think I can be saved?" I asked in a small voice.

"I'm betting my life on it," Mond said seriously. The rush of his fire propelled us on in the silent night. "Because if you're going, I'm going. It's a packaged set. Me and you. Can't live without your heart, right?"

I wriggled into him. He whimpered a bit as I crushed my

face into his neck, but he pushed back. I pulled away before I hurt him.

If this worked, there was plenty of time for that later.

We flew across the ground, watching as water skimmed underneath, and then woods. Finally, a cityscape started showing. New York?

We stayed near the top of the buildings, trying to keep hidden. The lights were enough to blind me as Mond fired us past the many lit signs.

One of the buildings held Molly.

As we flew, suddenly, Mond stopped. He set us down in a building-top garden with lots of grass and trees. All of it blocked the humongous opening that was in the roof. It went straight down into the building, with walkways and stairs all the way down.

"Now we walk," Mond said. "She's down there. But we need to find the machine."

I pulled on his arm. "No, we need to stop Molly. For good. You have no idea the number of crimes she's responsible for."

He pressed one finger down my jawline, tender, full of sorrow. "I know. I read your diary. You have had so much pain."

"We need to stop her. Besides, I don't like the idea of searching for my salvation before liberating the building. We have no idea the defenses down there."

Mond knew I made sense. Just like him. He thought he could just find the secret hideout and then I'd be alive again. No searching. No fighting. "You're so silly," I whispered.

Suddenly, the noise of a loud helicopter made us spin around. I was ready for anything.

But I wasn't ready for Natalie and Erin to drop down first, followed by the rest of our team.

"Taking it right to the evil one's lair," Cindy said with a laugh. "Bold yet stupid, especially with no backup."

"What is this? You were freeing facilities." I couldn't fathom what was going on.

"You had your lies," Natalie said. "I had mine. Truth is, the ones at the facilities now are only thirteen or younger. They have time. You don't. Because you're utterly moronic. I traced Redmond, even as he traced you."

Mond's jaw dropped. "I was molten fire!" he exclaimed.

Natalie laughed. "Check your sock. My ice doesn't melt."

Mond leaned down and flicked a small diamond of ice out of his sock. "Great. So much for secrets."

"Secrets are dangerous," Natalie scolded. "But we've gotten this far. Oh, and you can thank Bobby for the theft of a helicopter. Turns out he always wanted to fly one."

He grinned at me from his spot inside the helicopter. "Cool, huh?" he yelled over the blades. "I think I like this idea better to get back and forth to the island. Or this place, if it is what Natalie says it is. You'll have to stay here, right?"

Great! Did everyone know my business?

Natalie smirked at me. She gestured for Bobby to fly the helicopter away after a minute or so. What she was waiting for baffled me. "He's our getaway if this goes badly. I hope you don't mind us coming along. Rust doesn't keep very good patient-doctor confidentiality. I had a feeling this was how this would happen. Redmond doesn't seem the type to give up."

I gave Doctor Smythe a glare. "Okay, fine. Then we're all together."

Rust nodded. "Yep. And trust me, you're going to need all of us to take this place down."

Somehow, I believed him. As I stared down the many levels, I could see Breathers and others scurrying around. A building full of roaches. We had to eradicate them.

"Shall we?" I asked.

My team... My friends nodded in unison.

I was going into battle again. But this time I was fighting for a lot more than freedom. I was fighting for my future. And Mond's.

CHAPTER 35

I am livid right now! I am being kept out of the battle. The liberation of this area isn't under my control. I was sure they'd let me come along. I mean, I was there. I have skills. It's been me the whole time.

But what did my traitorous boyfriend do? He gave me my diary and said, "Go ahead and write while we kick ass."

I was about to say, "Yeah, sure," but then Erin grabbed me from behind, lifted me up, and Cindy helped her throw me into the helicopter, which had just conveniently returned.

It turns out I wasn't the only one with a secret plan.

According to them, I might drain myself beyond help. And that's why they were there, blah, blah, blah!

Bobby is giving me small waves from across the helicopter. We landed on another roof, hoping no one would mind. So far, so good. But it's driving me crazy. I can't believe they would do this!

Okay, fine, I was almost out. One very big explosion would have me gone.

Too big of a risk. I get it.

But this is my thing! I was the one who returned to the facility and saved them all. Fine, I'll be honest, Diary and Mond. I only went back because of Mond.

But it kills me that I am out of the story. Not even able to watch. Bobby is interrupting me, and I am ignoring him. He tossed me some Cheetos. My one weakness, before I couldn't really eat, that is.

My dress is impractical to let me eat or sit comfortably. Hey, I was going into battle. That worked well, then.

I'm... I'll admit it. I'm scared. Mond could die. Natalie. Erin. Cindy. Now, I guess I know how they felt when they found out what I was doing.

Just desserts taste awful!

Bobby just stiffened. He's talking. Oh, he has the earpiece. They're telling him what's going on.

Let me turn over to a report, Diary, because Bobby's telling me what's going on as I sit here.

They went down the stairs, hitting the first walkway. Cindy and the other Ice Burners made a wonderful icy staircase that led down, down, down.

Riders attacked right away.

Argh! This is so frustrating. It's like a third-person radio report. Okay, let me try again.

Redmond jumped down with his form fully flamed. He's so good. As he fell, he burned all the staircases so no one could retreat.

It didn't take long before Molly came out with her malfunctioning suit.

Bobby's laughing. "Natalie is gloating about how utterly she surprised her sister," he just informed me. I am giving him the "stick to the facts" glare. He got it.

They're all resorting to physical fighting.

Redmond is fire-punching some Breathers. One, two, three.

Damn it! Bobby sounds like a fight announcer. Oh, ow. He's taking it on the chin!

Great. I'll keep going. I can do nothing else. All I am is my ears, listening to what's happening. Wondering about the news. The helicopter is dimmed around me. All I see is Bobby's chin moving.

Natalie is in her ice form again. She and Redmond are battling back-to-back. Everyone else is using any weapons they brought.

A gun went skittering. Cindy lost it.

She jumped into the air, using an ice pillar under her feet.

I remember that, Diary. Having ice. Funny, in this space, where Bobby is silent, waiting for the next report, I realize what they're all fighting for. The chance for me to return to my Ice Burner status.

For me. It hurts. It feels great. It's both. Like a sword that cuts and heals at the same time. I could be healed. I could be back. It had been such a short time without my ice, but it felt like forever. Like there was never a time when I wasn't dying. When I wasn't sizzling like a live wire.

Bobby is speaking again.

They cleared the area. Molly is hovering overhead. The Riders or Breathers have fled. Go, team!

Bobby is silent again. He cast a look at me.

Oh. It's not going well.

Bobby is speaking slow. I'm going to dictate exactly what he says.

"They're surrounded. Molly is spitting missiles like a waterfall throws water. Cindy and the other Ice Burners have erected an ice shield, but our people are retreating. And..."

Bobby shook his head and started flipping switches. He was going to take off. He's not saying anymore. Let me ask.

I can't believe this. I thought Bobby was being told to pick them up, but he's retreating.

Gotta go. Gotta sacrifice myself for my friends. I should have known this wouldn't end with me being happy. I am never happy long.

232

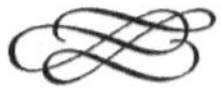

CHAPTER 36

I slammed the door of the helicopter open and burst into electricity.

"No, Laoni! What are you doing?" Bobby yelled as the blades started taking us up.

"I'm going back. Bobby, we're not leaving them!"

"But you'll die. Natalie said very clearly…"

I didn't wait to find out. I was zipping across the buildings. I caught my appearance. I didn't even look human anymore. Just a ball of light.

I knew where the building was. I skimmed through the open hole, watching the battle below.

Molly was breaking through.

"Not so fast!" I yelled and got in her way. "You're dead, do you hear me?"

Molly shot me a look. "Stop me before I kill them then if you're so freaking good. Do it! I will rip the skin from their bones."

The ice shield shattered. The missiles launched before I could even blink.

And I exploded. For the third time. Hitting everything

inches from my friends. Molly's suit crumbled into nothing, and she fell. Far. Long. Her body thudded at the bottom. Her missiles were gone.

My eyes were going dark.

Another thud should have happened. My body falling lifelessly. But once again, I was surrounded by heat.

But I was gone. My heart slowly stopped...my mind... shut...down.

CHAPTER 37

REDMOND

Her body seemed dead. My Laoni. Completely gone. Only black hair left. No white. Nothing. Her beautiful dress floated in the water, moving with whatever was powering the current inside. I stood still and waited. She was surrounded by some gelatinous liquid. Her hair floated freely inside of it. Her face was pale.

"Should we even bother?" Erin said next to me. She and I had first watch. To keep an eye on whether anything was changing. Both of us had blankets on makeshift beds to spend the night near Laoni. I didn't need mine. I couldn't even do anything but stare at her eyes, waiting for them to flicker. "This is what was supposed to happen. It always ends this way."

"Shut up," I said.

"Redmond!" Erin said and pushed her blankets off and stood up. Her eyes were blank. It was hurting her too. So did not care. "You did your best. You gave her your breath, pressed on her heart. I almost thought you were going to revive her. But look at her. That is a body."

Erin yelped as a tendril of my fire leaped at her. "Hey!"

"*Shut up!*" I hissed. "*She'll come back. I know she will. I won't give up. You're bored? Go.*"

Erin surprised me and put a gentle hand on my shoulder. She was lucky. Even with her control of fire, mine burned hotter, especially now. The glass around Laoni's crystal tomb reflected our faces. Two haggard and lost individuals. Our heart gone.

The team was all asleep now, but even with this kickass new place to hide out and continue our war from, we seemed to have lost our center. We didn't know which way to go. Even Natalie, our leader, was lost. We were supposed to save Laoni!

That was the whole point of this, why we kept her out of battle. Then she came back. Molly was gone. We had won.

But only because of Laoni's sacrifice. Now, how the hell were any of us supposed to continue on knowing that?

"Mond," Erin said.

I turned on her, my eyes blazing. I was ready to kill her. "Don't call me that."

"Sorry. I thought I heard Laoni... Never mind. I miss her too."

"As what? Someone to get into an argument with? Someone to tell how bad the world is? Someone to blame for the death of your ooey gooey parents!"

Erin slapped me. Hard. I deserved it. But I didn't rescind my statement.

She turned around and walked out. I was alone. I liked it better that way. They were all mourning a friend. But I was mourning... No! She wasn't dead. I was missing a part of my soul. I was supposed to die with her. But she saved us all. Me included.

"Redmond."

Great. No one got the point that I wanted to be alone. "What?" I spit at Natalie. She looked older.

"Her family wants the next watch," she said gently. She gestured as Drake, Gem, and Cher entered.

I looked around. It was a relatively huge room, made completely of white. There were large sets of some kind of equipment, mechanical, frozen areas. Lots of stuff. Had no idea what they were. "There's plenty of floor." I pointed to the little sleeping area we had made up.

"Maybe you should leave them to it," Natalie said.

I barked a laugh out and walked closer to Laoni. Her family could be here, but I wouldn't leave her. Never.

"Redmond, it's important for you to..."

My response was short and sweet. I erected my fire form. No one could touch me or even stand near me for long. I wasn't leaving. I felt the energy burning hot. I could keep this going for a very long time. I wasn't like Natalie, whose ice form drained her. I'd keep it up forever.

"Okay, I get it. Be stubborn," Natalie spit and walked out. I was pissing off all the women today.

"Over here?" Cher said.

I ignored her.

"She won't give up," a voice said next to my shoulder. I looked down and saw Gem. She wasn't at all put off by my fire. Ah, the Breather in her. Whatever.

Besides, she was saying something I loved. "You think so?"

Gem gave me a tentative smile. She was nervous around me. I had taken her off guard with the beauty of my wonderful Burner form, and she was still quite shy. She had Laoni's smile. I couldn't be angry at her.

"My sister survived years and years in a Burner facility. Survived years on the run. She found all of us. She won't just die. People like that don't just die. Death's not in her destiny. No..." She gazed at Laoni's form. Nothing changed. "She'll live."

I decided to say the same thing people kept telling me. Not to hurt her, but to have her refute them. Right now, Gem was the closest thing I had to Laoni. And if Laoni were able, she'd be making me feel better. "Her pulse is practically nonexistent. Better than when she fell, but there. They say that's not enough. Laoni's in a coma, and she's still dying from her powers."

Gem shook her head obstinately. "No. If she were in a normal hospital, she'd be dying. But the machine is giving back, not stealing from her."

"It's known as the Burner Augmenter 300," I said.

Gem nodded. "You saved her life."

Man, oh man, if only I could believe that. I stared harder than I ever had, looking for proof of Gem's statements.

But I saw nothing.

We all settled down, and I finally let my flames flicker out. No one seemed to want to kick me out now. Smart.

As I drifted off to sleep, I heard Gem's words again, "You saved her life... Death's not in her destiny."

My heart was wooden right now. Eaten away by my own flames. Those statements quenched my fire. She wasn't going to die.

I had gotten to her in time. Hadn't I?

Hadn't I saved her life?

Sleep claimed me.

I was awakened by a shrill shriek.

Gem was shaking my arm and running around to wake her parents as well. "Her hair! Her hair is white!"

EPILOGUE

REDMOND

aoni's hair was indeed white. One strand. But the machine was doing its job. Now the most annoying thing happened. Now that she was not dying or dead but living and, uh, recuperating, Natalie had no patience for me standing and staring at my girl all day and all night.

Worse, I had no excuses now. Natalie pulled a good one on me. "If she's not dying, she doesn't need you there all the time, unless you think she is going to die still."

I didn't think that! I had hope again. Her pulse was growing stronger. Her hair was a measure of her ice's return. My heart beat steadily because I knew Laoni was going to be fine.

But that meant I had to get back to work. The facilities still needed to be freed. Just because the leader was dead didn't mean what she had put in place was gone too.

There were still a lot of questions. Erin's siblings lived among us now, but I could swear sometimes they stopped moving, stared off into space, and clicked a few times. Did their Flyer addition get to them? If so, we had an enemy on the inside.

For once, Erin wasn't as pessimistic about them. She refused to believe they were anything but recovering. Though, I wondered.

And there was more. Rumors of Neo Breathers showing up. New Breathers. Riders. The reports were coming in.

I had no idea on what to think. We had won. Laoni had almost sacrificed herself to save us. Had that only been a cog in a bigger machine? Had Molly been our only threat?

Only time will tell.

But as I read Laoni's diary and saw how much she had gone through and was still kicking, I knew there was no threat we couldn't stop.

Someday, Laoni would be full strength again. She'd have her ice, so she would be able to create again. We'd be able to touch.

That was all that mattered.

We kept up our work.

Because there was time. An armistice.

Somehow, I knew that when Laoni did wake up, she'd come back to a bigger war than ever before.

For now, I'd let her rest.

I waited.

BURNOUT

books2read.com/burner3

In a world ravaged by time and teetering on the edge of annihilation, Laoni must confront a devastating truth: even the strongest ice can crack...

The future is a desolate wasteland, haunted by the absence of humanity. Evil creatures scour the skies, hunting down the remnants of a war that obliterated everything. Determined to uncover the dark secrets that led to this catastrophic downfall, Laoni embarks on a harrowing quest to unravel the mysteries of her decimated world and the enigmatic enemy responsible for its demise.

Caught between the past and the future, Laoni's extraordinary journey will right past wrongs and unravel the very fabric of time. Yet, there are rules governing her perilous endeavor. With only seven chances to set things right, failure is not an option. Each misstep brings her closer to a grim reality—a future forever scarred by destruction.

As the mystery of the enemy who triggered the world's demise deepens, failures and setbacks chip away at the remaining chances Laoni possesses. Bound by the inexorable march of time, every step she takes leads her closer to the fateful day when destruction's course is set in stone. And in that moment, there will be no second chances.

ABOUT THE AUTHOR

Marianna Palmer is a creative force who has been crafting captivating stories from the depths of her imagination since she first learned to dream. Encouraged by a dare from her sister, she bravely embarked on a journey into the world of writing, which became her sanctuary during years of solitude, personal challenges, and overcoming deep-rooted fears.

With an unwavering passion for storytelling, Marianna pursued her education and proudly earned her BA degree. However, she didn't stop there. Preferring the enigmatic allure of privacy, she briefly disappeared from the public eye, resurfacing intermittently in the company of her sister before once again retreating into her world of words.

Currently residing in the vibrant city of Tacoma, WA, Marianna draws inspiration from the beauty of her surroundings while reveling in the safety of her sister's presence. Determined to live life to the fullest, she fearlessly confronts the unknown, defying the daunting obstacles that once hindered her path.

https://mariannapalmer.wixsite.com/website

twitter.com/MariannaPalme18
instagram.com/mariannapalmerauthor
tiktok.com/@mpalmerwrites
bookbub.com/authors/marianna-palmer